RIFT

EGMONT PRESS: ETHICAL PUBLISHING

Egmont Press is about turning writers into successful authors and children into passionate readers – producing books that enrich and entertain. As a responsible children's publisher, we go even further, considering the world in which our consumers are growing up.

Safety First
Naturally, all of our books meet legal safety requirements. But we go further than this; every book with play value is tested to the highest standards – if it fails, it's back to the drawing-board.

Made Fairly
We are working to ensure that the workers involved in our supply chain – the people that make our books – are treated with fairness and respect.

Responsible Forestry
We are committed to ensuring all our papers come from environmentally and socially responsible forest sources.

For more information, please visit our website at
www.egmont.co.uk/ethicalpublishing

Beverley Birch

RIFT

EGMONT

For my daughters, Kate and Rachel

EGMONT
We bring stories to life

First published 2006
by Egmont UK Limited
239 Kensington High Street, London W8 6SA

Text copyright © 2006 Beverley Birch
Cover illustration copyright © 2006 Hannah Barton

The moral rights of the author and illustrator have been asserted

ISBN 978 1 4052 1589 3
ISBN 1 4052 1589 5

3 5 7 9 10 8 6 4

A CIP catalogue record for this title is available from the British Library

Printed and bound in Great Britain by the CPI Group

first day: waking

second day: Chomlaya

third day: footprints

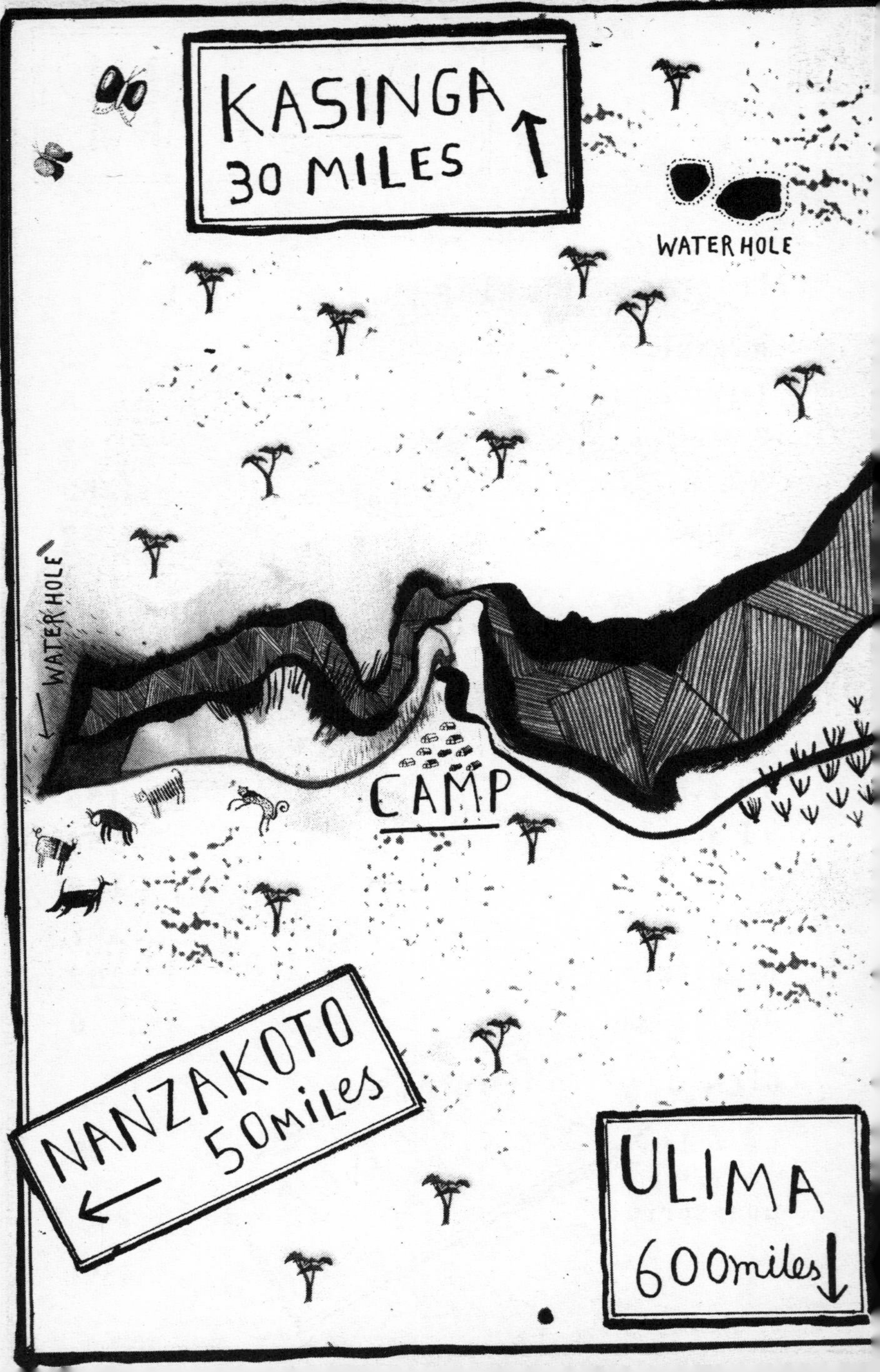
KASINGA
30 MILES
WATER HOLE
WATER HOLE
CAMP
NANZAKOTO
50 miles
ULIMA
600 miles

N
Area MAP
CHOMLAYA ROCKS
STREAM
LENGOI →
HOT SPRINGS
BURUKANDA
20 Miles

first day: waking

darkness

Ella turned her head, listened. Only the faint tick of her wristwatch in the heavy silence, and the boy's quiet presence. Darkness, thick and hot.

The boy had not moved: she was mistaken. Stiffly, she shifted her legs. Knotted muscles throbbed. She was sweating, yet cold.

How many hours till dawn?

She rolled over. Her eyes, travelling the dark, found the pale square of the newspaper. It lay on the floor beside her camp-bed, next to the backpack and shoes. She couldn't see the headline, but she didn't need to. She knew it by heart.

Front page, main story:

MIRACLE RESCUE OF MISSING BOY
Mystery deepens in 'Chomlaya Vanishings'
Missing British schoolboy, Joe Wilson, 14, has been found alive by young goat-herds at the base of Chomlaya Rocks.

Joe disappeared two days ago from his camp at the southern base of Chomlaya. Two other young British visitors, Matt Fisher and Anna Benham, and a local boy, Silowa

Asumoa, disappeared at the same time. British journalist Charlotte Tanner, 29, also vanished some time that day. It is not known whether the two events are linked.

Children tending goats spotted Joe wandering in a dry river gully which descends from the steep north slope of Chomlaya. District Commissioner James Meshami told us, 'It is many days' travel from the students' camp at the south of the precipitous ridge. We do not know how the boy could have reached the other side of Chomlaya, over such difficult and dangerous terrain.'

Joe was flown by helicopter to the nearest hospital at Nanzakoto township, fifty miles west of the camp.

Mystery deepens

Hopes of clues to the location of the others have collapsed, however, as Joe has no memory of the past few days.

Not a single trace of the other three youngsters or the journalist has been found. Police, game rangers and scores of local people continue to scour the area.

In an effort to widen the search, the government has announced that two more army helicopters will be deployed and a senior detective, Inspector Simo Murothi, is being sent in to help the local team led by DC Meshami.

Pictures, possibilities – terrifying possibilities – swarmed through Ella's mind. She forced her gaze away from the newspaper. She fixed on the sound of the boy's slow breathing: the one thread of hope, this stranger asleep in the bed across the hospital room.

Joe woke. A river of sound surged round him, vast, wild. Yet already it was dying, no more now than the slow, soft ebb of a distant tide . . .

He sat up. His throat was raw. His tongue traced his lips – dry blisters, cracked sores – he wondered at it, longed for water, wondered too at the small dark room cut by a shaft of moonlight through the window, crossing the floor and striping his sheets.

He turned his head. There was a camp-bed against the wall, the shadow of someone on it. He tried to fix its meaning in his mind, failed.

He fell back again and closed his eyes.

Ella heard Joe move. She sat up.

In the sudden wash of moonlight she could see his skin damp with sweat, bruises and scratches on his outflung arm. She eased herself off the camp-bed and went across to him, bent down, peered into his face. But he was still, seemed to sleep again, and there was nothing for her to do.

A renewed, bleak terror rose – for this boy, rescued, but from what? For her sister, missing. For the others, missing.

For herself.

In sleep, she thought, the boy looks so young, younger than he is, younger than me, and he isn't. She had the urge to touch him, to somehow soothe him as if he was a small child, as she wished someone would soothe her, stroking everything frightening away.

Does he know what's happened? Is he remembering, after all?

She returned to the camp-bed. She lowered herself on to it, carefully, not wanting the creak or the scrape of the metal legs on the concrete floor to wake him.

Joe's eyes snapped open. A shadow had touched his face. He lifted his head: only the rush of clouds across the sky, shrouding the moon, passing . . . moonlight repaints the room, white bands rippled by the fitful pattern of trees.

He felt a coldness now, a darkness nudging from memory, a glimmer of shape and shadow and flame –

The echo swirls from the dark like the stroking wings of an

insect, a boundless, urgent murmuring; he knows only its rhythm, the beat of his own heart, and the vast, soaring stillness beyond . . .

first light

Already the sky was paling. Hesitant bird cries sharpened Ella's restlessness. She threw back the covers, leaned down and searched for the notebook in her bag on the floor.

The photo came to hand first. Inspector Murothi had given it to her yesterday. She tilted it to catch the faint light from the window, and studied it again.

Two faded green tents. Grass, trees – and beyond, the glint of water and yellowing reeds.

In the foreground, two boys. The boy here in the hospital bed is one: *Joe*. The second is also one of the missing English students. Both pose, laughing for the camera, gazing at distant frontiers, hands shading eyes, packs shouldered.

Behind, two people sit cross-legged on the grass by the tents. They face each other: English girl and lanky, long-haired African boy. The girl's face, turned slightly to one side, is unnaturally bleached by the harsh glare of the sun. The contours of the boy's features are lost in shadow on his dark skin and he looks down at something small lying on the paler palm of his hand. The girl's looking at the object too, her hand is underneath his, as if steadying it; with one finger of the other hand she seems to touch the shape: there's that tilt of her head, as if she's thinking about it, as if she's on the point of speaking. Everything about these two suggests a taut, private alliance, uninterrupted by the antics of the others. Or by the approach of the woman walking between the tents. Though if you look closely you can see that she's gesturing at them, probably talking. Short, bushy fair hair, baggy trousers, so familiar, so recognisable . . .

Charly.

Yesterday, showing her the photo, telling her that this was all of the five people who went missing, all together, the inspector had tapped the faces one by one, named them: the English students – Joe, Matt, Anna. The African boy, Silowa. And at the back, the journalist, Charlotte: *I am told this is your sister, Miss Tanner,* he'd added. *Let me say to you that I am most extremely sorry.*

Charly.

It's important, this photo, Ella thought. She'd said that to the inspector. But he'd answered: *friends take pictures of each other, do you not think, Miss Tanner? I am not sure a photograph made weeks ago is of particular importance in these peculiar events.*

'Peculiar events'. The inspector's phrase nagged at her, and his face after he'd said it, snapping his mouth shut as if he regretted the words.

It *is* important! He's got to see. I've got to get to Chomlaya, so *I* can see!

She sat up. She swung her feet to the ground. She slipped the photo into the pages of her notebook and put it on her pillow, ready. She found her washing things, clean clothes, got up and went out into the corridor looking for a bathroom. She washed, changed, returned. Wondered whether to go in search of the nurse or the doctor to ask what would happen to Joe today. Catch them before the hospital clinics begin: on the way in yesterday, with the inspector, she'd seen the crowds. Afternoon: clumps of people sitting and leaning in deep shadows along outer walls. Waiting and waiting and waiting. Some of them walked days to get here, the inspector said, maybe fifty, sixty miles across plains, across relentless, waterless scrubland. He'd ushered her through them. She'd felt wrong, conspicuous, awkward. *Unfair.* Wanting to say *I'm not jumping queues, not taking anyone's place – just here to visit the English boy who was lost.* They eyeing her, expressions unreadable.

But not unfriendly, it occurred to her now. Not hostile. Curious, maybe, knowing; maybe they know why I'm here, maybe everyone knows, like they know why Joe's here, and the stranger policeman: Inspector Murothi come all the way up from the city.

She pushed the window wide. Outside the air was crisp. A light breeze carried a quickening chorus of birdwhistles and chirrups and throaty chuckles from the scrubby bush beyond the hospital grounds. Yellowing grass flanked a dirt road from the hospital to the narrow tarmac strip that was the main road north through Nanzakoto. A lone herdsman crossed the junction. The red dawn glow struck a glint from the point of his spear, and bony cattle ambled about the empty road ahead of him.

Her gaze moved beyond, above the fringe of trees and the scatter of homes, to the blue-silver haze of the plain. But it would change, fast: yesterday she'd seen it burning rust-red to the walls of the distant, sculpted rock-face of Chomlaya.

Up there, the search went on, helicopters going all through the night. 'New hope,' Inspector Murothi had said. He meant since they'd found Joe yesterday. He'd said it like a promise: *New hope for your sister, Miss Tanrer.*

A memory cut in: last night, a young nurse bringing her to this room, *We must put you here with this boy, because there is no other place for you. This boy is apart in a room we keep for visiting doctors, because the police did not want anyone to speak to him until they learned what he remembered by himself.*

Why? Ella had asked. *What do they suspect?* The nurse just pursing her lips in a wordless answer that Ella couldn't even begin to read.

The memory spiked a prickle of fear. The inspector thought Charly and the others were just lost, not *taken* by anyone? Didn't he?

Loud in the quiet room, Joe turned over, kicked off his sheets. They slid slowly to the floor. Ella lifted them, covered him, wished he'd wake so they could talk.

Instead she was left to fold up the bedding on the camp-bed. She rolled up the clothes she had travelled in from London and had now slept in. She pushed them into her pack. Then she took her notebook from the pillow and went to sit on the window-sill where the dawn light was strengthening.

Joe senses her there. He senses the room, and the rising chorus of birds, and the brightening air. But he is moving beyond, into dark – into the rising murmur, into the pulse of the darkness, into the beat of his own heart, into the vast, calling echo beyond.

Inspector Simo Murothi scraped the chair back and stood up.

The yellow lamp-glow had obscured the arrival of daylight, but he was aware suddenly of the strip of brightness beneath the door. He needed to escape the rumpled bed, used for a few hours before his somersaulting brain had forced him up; the police files on the table, the morass of fact and speculation about these inexplicable Chomlaya vanishings. And escape his worrying about the young English girl, Ella, he had left in the hospital.

He had persuaded the nurses to lodge her for the night. But what now, what today and tomorrow and the day after that? What did you do with a foreign child, an *orphan* foreign child, just fourteen years old, flying 6,000 miles from home, alone, on an impulse, into the middle of Africa? Such foolishness! Such *obstinacy*. He'd had to wrestle the truth out of the child!

Who knows you are here?

I left a note for my friends.

What about your family?

Charly's here.

Yes, of course, Miss Tanner, but I mean your family at home.

There isn't any.

Where are they, then?

They aren't anywhere.

I do not understand.

I live with Charly.

No one else?

My mum and dad are dead.

Ah! Ah! I am sorry – I am very sorry –

They were in a car accident when I was seven.

And so now you live with your sister?

*Well, see, Charly was twenty-two when it happened, and she
wanted to look after me, so they let her.*

And your sister is twenty-nine now?

Yes.

*So what happens when your sister – Charly – when Charly is
away working? Like now.*

*There's our friends, Holly and Christine. Holly's my best
friend, Christine's her mum.*

So they come to stay with you?

No, see, they live next door . . .

Challenging him, all the time. That direct, unblinking
stare daring him to send her back.

A nightmare, this Chomlaya case! Wandering orphans
looking for only sisters. Thirty British youngsters, a handful of
teachers, at the foot of a wild rock-face, in the middle of a hot,
arid plain, a day's driving at least from the nearest road.
What are you doing there? he wanted to demand. Apart from
losing people? The police enquiries so far did not tell him,

not really, not in a way that *satisfied*.

He pulled the room door wide. It brought a flood of bright warmth, dawn air spiced with a lingering dewy dampness. He ducked below the overhang of the veranda roof and stepped out into the compound. The square of beaten earth was neatly swept, empty, except for the flagpole spearing upwards, silhouetted against the rim of the sun and topped by the still, hunched figure of a crow. Below, the flag hung motionless. Not a breath of wind, not a breath of sound: his own footfall on the earth was an intrusion.

Suddenly, this unnerved Murothi. Where he came from, police stations were always open, a constable on duty at least. Here, no one moved in the sleeping quarters or the small stone building of the police station – office and cell. Even the dogs were silent. Maybe he was alone here, in a place where policemen expected not one single problem during the long hours of darkness and went comfortably home, letting trouble wait till the morning. Maybe he was *imprisoned* here, in a half-world between night and day, until someone chose to rescue him!

He was stooping slightly. He straightened to his full height. Murothi, you become ridiculous, he rebuked himself. Always, you leap to stupid thoughts! Of course these people will ignore you. They think you are a big puff adder lying in their path. They do not disturb you in case you bite. District Commissioner Meshami's face had said it: 'We will find these vanishing foreigners without upstart outsiders like you, sent by the Minister. Do not hurry into *my* place, Inspector Murothi, to prove your cleverness and the stupidity of the police of the Northern Province.'

Vanishing foreigners. Murothi turned and looked east, into the flare of the climbing sun. Somewhere in that immense wild place below, four people had utterly vanished. At some time no one could pinpoint. For reasons no one could guess.

Be quick, Murothi! the Minister had instructed. *Silence the newspapers.* Vanishing foreigners meant Falling Tourist Bookings and Wild Speculation: animals, snakes, kidnap, armed gangs, ivory poachers, a rogue army unit from across the western border . . .

Be quick! How? Snap his fingers, like some god, and the lost will be found?

'Why me?' he had asked. 'That Chomlaya place is not my place. I do not understand it. There is the District Commissioner there. There are the game rangers there. *They* know that place –'

But you are very clever with journalists. Very clever with hysterical relatives.

But what if the story is bad? Murothi thought. What if the story is just bad?

Sitting at the hospital window, Ella stared at her notebook, still empty. She'd meant to shape the clutter of questions in her head into some kind of plan. Instead, yesterday crowded in: the airport in Ulima; the taxi launched like a battering ram through thick city traffic; its driver, fretting: *The search for vanished people is famous! In the newspaper I read it! You must go to the police post, I will take you fast, straight now!* Escorting her in, pushing her to the enquiry desk, tapping for attention, drawing only the disdainful glare of the policewoman: *I know nothing; I hold out no hope.*

That apology on the taxi driver's face! She'd trailed him back to the door, struggled to make sense of the coins, let him pick them from her palm, show her, squealing at the tip she offered: *No, no! SUCH a child you are! DO NOT BE SO FOOLISH! To come to this country alone! You must pay just the fare or you will have no money, you must not be CARELESS like this! Wait here, wait, talk to the policemen.* Thin, elderly, he'd climbed stiffly into his taxi, nudged it back into the clatter of the street, swung out of sight. And for a moment, aloneness had paralysed her. She'd forced herself back to the waiting-room where people wandered in and out, slept on benches, the place heavy with a sultry, drifting mood that said there'd be days and days spent here –

The notebook pages blurred. Nothing to write. Chomlaya, *Chomlaya*. Inspector Murothi's got to take me there. Then I can *do* something, look for Charly, *find* her.

Half past six: two hours before he'd return to the hospital. Joe still asleep. She looked at him lying facing her, blind to her presence.

She shuffled back on the window-sill and drew her knees up, propping the notebook open. She'd bought it weeks ago, to write a diary of the visit Charly'd planned, the two of them travelling together when the student camp at Chomlaya was over –

Together.

Skittering from the thought, she scribbled quickly:

27 February

Well, here I am – Nanzakoto Regional Hospital. It's hundreds of miles north of Ulima where I landed yesterday, and it feels like a century later. I keep thinking, what if Charly and me HADN'T already got the visa and passport and stuff sorted for when I'm SUPPOSED to be here WITH HER? What if people had INSISTED on knowing why I wanted to change the ticket and who was meeting me? What if I'd had to say, my sister's VANISHED, I'm just going to find her.

Don't know what I'd have done if they'd stopped me! But there I was on the plane, taking off — 11 in the evening, 8 hours flying ahead, we were in the air, they were turning the cabin lights down, and all around me people just went to sleep! It got quieter and quieter and quieter, and that's when I REALLY saw what I'd done! I just sat there, wide awake and thinking, thinking, wondering, wondering. What did they MEAN, your sister's disappeared? What did they MEAN, 'continue to hope'? 'We'll let you know'!!! What did they expect me to do — just hang about, waiting?

I remember the captain telling us that we were crossing the coast of North Africa. But I couldn't see anything — just blackness outside, and the horrible gloominess inside, and then I MUST have gone to sleep, because next thing the whole cabin glowed, the sun was a great fire on the horizon, even the wing of the plane seemed to burn. We were already low, crossing forest along the coast. Then we circled out over the sea and back, and came in along a narrow strip of land to the airport.

Charly, if this was the holiday we meant, if I was coming to join you like we planned, if I wasn't here because you're LOST, I'd have been so excited. I could just see Ulima ahead — palm trees and white buildings and purple flowers, it looked fantastic in the pink light – magical – and the sea was deep blue with frothy white sandy edges, just like all the pictures you showed me. I don't know what I expected, but we got off the plane and it was steamy-hot, sticky-damp, slow and sleepy. Then it was such a shock because you'd written about the dry, baking kind of heat at Chomlaya, choking dust, drought, I remember you called it PITILESS, and somehow finding this instead was like I'd come to the wrong place by mistake, and I felt really afraid, sort of swirling inside, and I had to remind myself it's the right place, just a different part of it.

And when everything seemed to take a hundred years (even the flies are half asleep), it was all like some weird hallucination, like watching a film of myself from a distance. The airport was still mostly shut, so it was an hour before I could ask anyone for help, and I still couldn't stop digging over what the people from your office said on the phone – what they HADN'T said. Wondered if I should ring them, but phoning all the way back to London now, when I'd already got here, just felt silly.

First discovery: no such thing as a regular plane to Nanzakoto, or anywhere near. I could charter a plane !!! Or 9 hours drive by 'taxi', or 2 or 3 days on buses. Then 5 or 6 more hours by Land Rover (IF you could find one to take you) from

Nanzakoto to your camp at Chomlaya Rocks.

I decided to go to the police station.

Second discovery! At the police station, everyone knew NOTHING about ANYTHING.

Ha! I was ready for that! My taxi driver TOLD me he saw it in the newspaper, so I knew I'd get an answer from SOMEONE. Didn't think of going to the British High Commission — don't know why (probably, deep down, knew they'd just send me back on the next plane). But after 4 hours I was giving up hope, worrying how I'd find somewhere to stay for the night. Don't have any kind of map (how stupid is that! You'll be furious with me when you find out!) I really wished I'd asked the taxi driver to come back for me — he would have, and he'd have taken me to an OK hotel, he was that kind of person.

Then, bang! Slamming doors, and a policewoman rushing out to find me. Turned out this new inspector had arrived, just been given the 'Chomlaya Case'. A few minutes talk with HIM, and he's rung the British High Commission to report I'm here (lectured me for not telling them — he sounded just like the taxi driver, all disapproving). And he made me own up about everything — he wanted to contact someone in England about me, so I had to tell about there being just you, and he got quiet and looked all shocked and worried. Then he made me explain how this time I wasn't actually staying next door with Holly and Christine at night, they were just keeping an eye on me, and I sneaked a note under their door when I left so they wouldn't see it till too late to stop me getting the plane. Then he started to get sort of angry – or it was frustrated, maybe – and gave me a lecture about the dangers of what I'd done, but then he stopped, and sort of looked at me, and said sorry, and went quiet all over again. And then told me about Joe being found, and went away and phoned lots of people, and then said he's taking me on the plane bringing him up here to Nanzakoto, and he showed me the English-language newspaper that said about Joe –

She'd become aware, slowly, of the rising drone of an aircraft. It struck her that it might be a helicopter heading for Chomlaya and she lifted her head, scanned the sky. But it was a large plane passing high overhead, moving steadily south, and she thought again of her own flight from London yesterday, wondered if she'd passed this close, even flown above the camp where Charly'd been. These distances had meant nothing to her before: she hadn't understood at all from Charly's letter and emails.

She slipped off the window-sill and went across to her pack. She unzipped a pocket, pulled out a wad of folded pages and returned to her seat in the light.

On top was Charly's first letter, dated more than two weeks ago, 9 February. The bit Ella remembered came near the end . . .

I keep wondering what these kids – city spirits, every one of them – are really going to make of all this. Just think – it's 600 miles from Ulima to Nanzakoto. Another 50 to the camp, but it might as well be 500 - straight across the plain, no roads – impassable in the rainy seasons, though baked dry now. Tracks like corrugated iron, so it's 4-wheel drive only. Some of the kids started moaning the moment we got off the tarmac. I swear, not an unbruised bone left in my body. Whole truck rattling to bits. Hot as hell – hotter!! Spied 1 human habitation in the whole brown expanse – maybe 20 homes inside a great barrier of thorn branches piled high. To keep out lion and leopard! You know, Elly, I read things like that, I see it in films, but I don't really grasp any of it. There's something terribly blinkered about that, isn't there – is it just me – maybe I don't have the imagination?

But then I do see it: people digging for water in a dried-up river bed. No other hint of water between leaving the tarmac road and reaching the camp. Tiny kids herding sheep and goats, miles and miles from any village. Bony-thin cattle running with zebra and wildebeest (like some weird prehistoric creature, all gangly and heavy-headed). I had a *sudden attack of nerves about this whole trip — about how superficial it'll be, really. I'm sure the kids will learn something (though I have my doubts about some of the teachers). When you talk about people enlarging their horizons and all such lofty intentions — it depends what you're prepared to see, doesn't it? I can think of at least three kids here who aren't going to see much beyond the tent they'll flop about in, the suffocating heat, the creepy-crawlies, the absence of running water to wash their hair. They'll complain endlessly of nothing to do. They'll spend a whole month here, and go away with no sense of place or person in the scheme of things, no sense of any of this place's LIFE (and death). I know it'll sound like a ridiculous cliché, but as we headed out over the plain towards Chomlaya Rocks, I had this sudden overwhelming picture of how weak and absurd we were, rattling along through this immensity in a rickety tin box . . .*

Ella lifted her eyes from the letter. She stared, unseeing, at the hospital grounds. She hadn't particularly recalled that last comment. Now it penetrated with unusual force. With it came a memory of yesterday: herself in the little four-seater plane flying from Ulima — Inspector Murothi and the pilot and her. She'd leaned her head against the window, watching mangrove swamps and lush coastal forests below give way to low hills, then to a canvas of tawny swirls and purple shadows, chains of narrow lakes studding the floors of flat brown valleys, a sweep of yellowing plain, ragged trees, gashes of raw red earth, like wounds. Finally they'd circled down towards the landing strip at Nanzakoto, the plane's shadow racing across the ground like a giant bird. There'd been a herd running below. But she'd not really been paying attention, eyes skimming ahead to the river and its sprawl of low buildings, to the knuckles of far-off mountains beyond. Then with a lurch of astonishment she'd grasped that the animals were not cattle. Zebra, antelope, giraffe scattered in a fast gallop, drifting to a halt as the plane banked away. She'd let out a cry – delight – amazement – shock – it was so close – and the inspector had glanced across the plane at her. 'Let me say this, Miss Tanner – in these regions people's lives are . . . *cheek by jowl* with the wild . . . That is, I think, how you could say it, in English –?'

A blare of sound snapped the memory, raucous cawing blasting from the roadway. A lone dog trotted along the metallic sheen of the tarmac. Gaunt, sway-backed, his long-legged, large-headed shadow paced below him like a monster-beast on crooked stilts. Languid on slow-beating wings, crows wheeled, dropped down, melted into the patchwork foliage of trees.

She thought suddenly of hyenas, wild dogs, vultures, and her heart pounded for Charly.

For several minutes, Joe had been watching her. She reminded him of Charly. But she was smaller, younger, and her hair was dark and long, not like Charly's short, fair –

The vision seeped through him gently – a flow of colour warming the still, quiet room. He saw Charly, Silowa: Charly kneels by the stream, rinses something, shakes droplets of water, inspects, dips again . . .

Shaded sand below trees – he remembers it soft, cool to the toes, pockmarked with birds' feet, ringed with reeds. They rustle like a whisper passed from leaf to leaf, and Charly turns, smiles, speaks. Silowa laughs, strides through water, patterns star-splashed in the dust on his legs, he leaps the bank into sunlight and the birds fan up, whirring blurs of brilliance, yellow birds, hundreds of yellow birds, making Anna duck, squeal, and Matt –

Police. Yesterday. *When did you leave the camp?* Police, yesterday, yesterday, yesterday. Here, in the hospital: he wrestled to keep hold of the knowledge.

. . . burning rock – great blunt fingers point to the sky, and Silowa's feet climb towards them, puffs of dust from his heels,

Anna chattering, like the chittering of monkeys above – quivering branches, sun flickers through leaves ... Matt scrambles, slithers, and Silowa shouts *Matt, here! Joe, up! Up, up!*

When did you leave the camp? Police. *Police* –

A soft, slight sound crossed the room. The girl – the shuffle of her moving. She was turning a page. She pushed hair off her face, tucked it behind her ears, stared into space, began writing again: write, think, write.

He looked round the room. He took in the camp-bed, the open backpack, sandals kicked off in the middle of the floor. He spread his hands on the mattress below him, found its edges, square, solid, *real*. He breathed the bright air that flowed through the window, saw, beyond the girl's head, that a bird rode the wind lazily across the sky –

... remembers the blue-orange blaze of a kingfisher skim the water – across, and back, and out again, everyone gathering firewood, fetching water, tents lifting, canvas billowing, hammers thudding, and that whirlwind of rainbow colour swoops down and away along the stream, and from somewhere else, somewhere high and beyond, a long, trailing cry rises to the crags –

No, Joe thought. *Not then. It wasn't then; was that later?*

struggling to order the pattern of days and failing.

Ella, sensing his gaze, turned and saw he was awake.

'Joe! Are you OK? I'll fetch the nurse —'

Joe shook his head. Partly saying no, partly warding off the half-remembered sounds, rising from nowhere, smudging all other thought. With effort, he sat up. He threw back the sheet. He put his feet to the floor and stood up, wincing in surprise at bruising, at toes that felt like pincushions. He sat down again, heavily.

Ella was hurrying towards him. 'Don't! They'll want you to stay in bed —'

'I'm OK.' He demonstrated, stretching against the shrieking stiffness of muscles in his back, stomach, legs, standing up again.

'Wait, I'll find the nurse . . .' Ella paused, he said nothing, and she rushed on, flustered now, because awake he no longer looked young, small, vulnerable, but was large, dishevelled, her own age, he wouldn't want her fussing — a stranger. 'Sorry — I slept here — I mean — well — the inspector said — everyone else's still at Chomlaya . . . you know . . .' She ended lamely, embarrassed at the avalanche of unnecessary gabble. 'I'm — I'm Charly's sister,' she blurted. 'Ella. I mean my name's Ella. I'll — I mean — oh, I'll go!'

Behind the hastily closed door, Joe sank to a sitting position, thankfully. The bombardment confused him. He focused hard: she looks like Charly because she's Charly's sister . . .

But other things came too – doctor, police, questions, questions, questions . . .

He stiffened, braced in case the door opened and it was them again, insisting, asking over and over, not believing that he *remembered* the night when they'd stayed in the tent. He could recall that so clearly, waiting in darkness, close, *from outside no one'll see we're here*, Anna'd whispered . . .

Then just children shrieking, small hands pulling, larger hands lifting him, water dribbled on his lips, children holding branches to shade him, swatting away flies, sighing and stroking his face, and the drone of a helicopter, black against scalding skies.

In between: nothing. Blank. Blank, blank, blank.

Do you understand, Joe, that your friends, Anna, Matt, Silowa – all your friends – are not at the camp? The journalist, Charlotte, is not at the camp. The words came to him in the measured tones of the policeman. As if explaining to someone stupid. The memory brought a clammy sweat and a churning somewhere deep in his gut.

He wished, suddenly, that the girl would come back. He wished he'd stopped her rushing off like that.

He got to his feet. He found his balance carefully, and made his way towards the door.

It snapped open. A nurse barred his way, half his height and twice his strength, sucking her cheeks in with disapproval, marching him back to bed, hijacking the next minutes with temperature and pulse-taking peppered with tongue-clicks of displeasure: at the marks on his legs, at the redness of his eyes, at whatever it was she read in the notes she carried on a clipboard, her face swept by concentration, puzzlement, irritation, finally, grudgingly, approval.

'You are rested,' she announced, gripping his wrist and pulling his arm out, then the other, turning each to and fro, inspecting briskly.

He said, 'It's only bruises.'

'I know this!' She flicked the clipboard with one finger. 'Dehydrated. Exhausted. And what is this nonsense?' She shoved the writing at him. He couldn't read it – all scrawls, and anyway it probably wasn't in English.

'Lost memory,' she enunciated each word separately, and sniffed. 'This ridiculous walk you have done! Do you leave your brains in England? *Wisdom* is needed to do these things. Tch!

Tourists! Now all these people must run about searching for you! How many people must spend their time rescuing wandering children when there is other urgent work to do? Where are your teachers? I ask you this! What are *they* doing while you go around and lose yourselves? Dismiss them all – this *I* would do. Tcchk – tcchk – gone!' With a flap of her hand she demonstrated them disappeared, and Joe didn't try to protest that he wasn't a child, hadn't *tried* to get lost, for the prospect of certain teachers *dismissed* was spiced with a satisfying tang of vengeance.

The nurse stood back. She tilted her head to one side, surveying him. Then she swung round and went to the door.

'The doctor will see you, when he is *free* to. *You* will wait here. Do *not* wander about like your friend. I cannot have strangers in my hospital getting "*lost*".' But the jibe was coloured by an unexpected, quick smile.

Through the door, briefly open as she left and clicked smartly shut behind her, he spied Ella being shooed away, *we are not a hotel!* When he yanked the door open again, there was no one in sight.

7 a.m.

Why is this boy, *Silowa*, at the Chomlaya camp? The question plagued Murothi. Silowa is not part of this foreigners' expedition. Yet he is a friend of those who disappeared. He disappears with them, all the evidence says this. How does he come there? Is the *how* significant? Murothi felt it was, but he did not know why.

He rubbed his hands across his face. Ah! To be waking in his own bed now, to have only the short walk to his own police post under the shade of the great fig tree! He had a sudden pang of guilt at the thought of Ella, waking alone in the hospital. *Two continents from her own home!* He could not imagine such a feeling. *It is not right to leave the child there*, he thought. *It is a cold thing I have done.*

He stood, gazing down from the police compound across maize fields falling towards the river. Tea shacks clustered at the crossing point, and beyond crouched the brown hulk of the ferry. On both sides Nanzakoto township straggled along the riverbanks, little more than a meeting place and market for the hundreds of families moving animals about the plains. Yet raised in importance because it also had the regional hospital and this police post, planted here because of the road and river crossing and the new landing-strip for small aircraft.

For all that, it was dwarfed by the immense, harsh sweep of the land, so unlike the moist green valleys of Murothi's own, distant, home. In truth, he was exiled here: the price of his overnight climb to 'Inspector'. Exile! In this place he could not *feel*. Until he found the vanished. *Repeat your success* the Minister instructed. But that 'success' was very different: a tourist disappearance on the coast last year. A murder hunt: a body, a culprit, evidence to be gathered. Nasty, but not complicated. Murothi had proved it was foreigner against foreigner. Sighs of relief all round: no dishonour to local people or Important Persons in charge of Tourist Places. Murothi's skills had been discussed in very high places!

He turned, and went back into the room, to the table with its spread of police files. This was different. Very different. Where, *how* to begin?

Certainly, the investigations on this Chomlaya case were thorough: searches – a thirty-mile radius, air and ground; scores of interviews. DC Meshami's team had talked to everyone at the camp, all six teachers, every one of the remaining twenty-seven students, the two wild-life rangers . . .

Painstaking work. Meticulous. *Laziness*, thought Murothi, is not why this Chomlaya case is unsolved. This DC Meshami is good. Good policemen work for him.

Yet nearly three days go by, and still four people are missing. A fifth reappears. Out of nowhere. Remembering nothing.

His eye fell on the interview transcript of one of the six British teachers, and he picked it up:

```
Ian Boyd (IB)
Date: 24/2/06
Time: 19.30
Place: Northern Province. Chomlaya, British Student
Camp
Interviewed by District Commissioner James Meshami
(DC), Constable Ndoto Lesakon (NL): Nanzakoto
Police Department.
Case No: 06574
Tape reference: 2006/Chomlaya/17
```

DC   Please explain your role here.

IB   I teach at Gresham Secondary School in London, where these students all come from.

DC   Do you know the missing students well?

IB   Yes. I teach Anna and Matt. I don't teach Joe now, but I did last year. And I know him from swimming club - he's a keen swimmer.

DC   Tell me your movements today.

IB   I was driving back from Lengoi Hot Springs with half the students. We camped overnight there. We got back here around five this afternoon -

DC   And you left Lengoi at what time? By what route?

IB   About eight this morning. We stopped several times on the way to let the students look around.

[Constable NL shows map to IB. IB traces route from Lengoi south across ford at Tumla River, approaching Chomlaya from east.]

DC   And just tell me - when did you first leave Chomlaya to go to Lengoi?

IB   Just yesterday morning. About ten-thirty.

DC   Were the missing students in the camp when you left?

IB   Definitely.

DC   You saw them?

IB   Yes.

DC   And Silowa?

IB   Yes.

DC   I understand he is not actually a member of your student expedition. But he was often here at the camp?

IB   He is friends with Anna, Matt and Joe - others,

too, but particularly those three.

DC And he was definitely here when your party left
for Lengoi? I am sorry to be so insistent on
this point -

IB Yes, yes, he was. Ask anyone.

DC So, did your group separate at all between your
departure for Lengoi yesterday morning and your
return to Chomlaya two and a half hours ago?

IB We were all together, all the time.

DC After we have finished speaking, please give
Constable Lesakon here the names of everyone
who went to Lengoi with you. But now, tell me,
what was the situation when you got back here
this afternoon?

IB We drove in. Some students came running out to
tell us what had happened. The four of them
could have been missing all day, all last night
too, for all anyone knew! We -

DC Who is 'we'?

IB Sorry, that's Helen, Keith, David, Tomis,
Likon, me - we organised a search. [Angry] I
just wish they'd stayed on the trip to Lengoi -

DC Who? What do you mean?

IB Joe, Matt and Anna - they were meant to come
with us. The students are divided into two
groups, you see. Fifteen in each. One group at

a time goes on a trip in the two Land Cruisers, the other group stays in camp. The students have named the groups the 'Buffalos' and the 'Antelopes'. Joe, Anna and Matt - they're in the Buffalos. The *Buffalos* went to Lengoi. But just as we were leaving, those three were told to get off the vehicle.

DC   Who by?

IB   Elisa Strutton, leader of the expedition.

DC   Why?

IB   She said they'd committed some misdemeanour -

DC   Had they?

IB   I doubt it, but we left for Lengoi before it was sorted out. I wanted to wait, but Helen and Keith were worried that if we delayed any more, we'd end up travelling after dark. It's a five-hour drive, minimum, you know - and there's no track till you get right up to the river. So three other students took the place of Anna, Matt and Joe, and off we went. We all wish we hadn't, in view of what's happened.

DC   So this teacher, Elisa Strutton, has ultimate authority?

IB   Appointed leader by the head teacher of the school.

DC   And these other names? Helen, Keith?

IB   Yes, that's the other teachers, Helen Milton and Keith Derby. We're all from Gresham School. David Ntanyaki, the driver, and Tomis Ntonye, the ranger - both local men, part of the expedition organisation. We all went to Lengoi. The Land Cruisers travelled together all the way. David drove one carrying seven students and me and Tomis, and Keith drove the other with eight students and Helen.

DC   When your vehicles arrived back here at Chomlaya, had there been any search for the missing students?

IB   No. Well, that's unfair. Likon was here, the other ranger. He'd been with some of the students on some activity along the stream, and as soon as he heard there were people missing, he organised a look round the area near the camp. Everyone assumed that Anna, Joe and Matt were just playing truant. A bit of panic was beginning, though. Lawrence, that's one of the teachers who stayed at Chomlaya, he was getting worried. And then no one knew where Charly was either.

DC   Charlotte Tanner, the journalist?

IB   Yes. She's documenting our time here for her magazine. She drove off to the archaeology camp

at Burukanda early yesterday to email her young
sister in England. She has particular friends
at Burukanda; you should talk to them -
Véronique and Otaka in particular.

DC   I know them. I will speak to them, thank you.
Now, we have been told that Charlotte came back
to Chomlaya.

IB   Yes, about midday, I gather. Just when everyone
realised Anna and the others weren't in camp.
But when I went looking for Charly, I couldn't
find her. I thought she might know if Anna and
the others had planned to go further afield
than usual. She knew them quite well, you see.
But she seems also to have disappeared!

DC   So, a serious search began only when you
returned from Lengoi? How long after you got
here?

IB   Twenty minutes, half an hour. Not more. But it
was soon clear we weren't going to find them
before nightfall on our own, so we persuaded
Elisa to radio for help. About then we worked
out Silowa was missing too. We're used to him
coming and going. I'd assumed he'd gone back to
Burukanda with Charly. But several of the kids
said he'd been in the camp with Joe and the
others last night, and that was long after

Charly drove away to Burukanda.

DC   This search - you were all involved?

IB   Yes, we broke up into parties of five or six students, each with a teacher. Each group covered a particular area - all along the paths the students generally use, and a short way out on to the open plain, but we were nervous of letting anyone out of our sight.

DC   Yes, understood. Well, that's all for the moment, Mr Boyd. Thank you. Please give Constable Lesakon that list of names. If you think of anything else, let us know without delay. We have little time, obviously.

IB   Are you interviewing all the teachers?

DC   Is there someone we should talk to particularly?

IB   No, I don't mean that. Just - you'll hear that these missing students are . . . problematic.

DC   Problematic?

IB   Troublesome. Wilful.

DC   And?

IB   It's not true.

DC   Who will say this?

IB   Some of the teachers. Two of the teachers, really. Elisa Strutton and Miss Hopper - she always agrees with Miss Strutton.

DC   You think it is not true?

IB   Look, these kids aren't fools, or always up to some mischief, as you'll be told. Whatever's happened won't be because they've been stupid, or gone looking for trouble.

DC   You have an idea what might have happened?

IB   No! Hell, I wish I did! Just. . . . I mean, these students, they're curious young people, in the best sense of the word. Eager. They share that with their friend, Silowa. Whatever's happened won't be because they've been deliberately *disobedient* - that's all I mean. Just wanted to say that.

DC   That is very helpful. Thank you.
      INTERVIEW ENDS 19.42

Thoughtfully, Murothi reread the last few answers. Then he looked for the DC's interview of the teacher in charge of the camp, Elisa Strutton. He found the first question about the missing students.

DC   When did you see them today?

ES   I haven't seen them.

DC   When did you last see them, then?

ES   Yesterday, at supper.

DC   Is it usual not to assemble the students at all

during the day?

ES   Everyone has assigned tasks in the camp. There is no need to assemble.

DC   What were Anna, Matt and Joe's tasks?

ES   Today, kitchen duties. Preparing the meals. That's why we knew they were not there. They did not prepare lunch. The camp cook is away today. Normally he would supervise this. I would have hoped that students could be trusted to get on with something like this without supervision, but clearly not.

DC   What were they supposed to be doing before the food preparation?

ES   They were given the task of digging a new trench.

DC   Where was this?

ES   At the back of the camp. For the toilets. The old trench was damaged during the storm three nights ago, the sides broke down. We need to fill it in and dig a new one.

DC   Who else was doing this?

ES   Just those three.

DC   What were other students doing?

ES   Various things.

DC   Please supply further details, in writing.

ES   I will ask one of the other teachers to give -

DC   I would prefer you to do it. As you are in charge, you understand. If you would be so kind. I will cross-check this with what was actually happening.

ES   Are you suggesting -?

DC   I am suggesting nothing. I am being thorough. Now, when did you last see Silowa?

ES   He is not supposed to be here. I have no responsibility for him.

DC   That is not my question. The students say he was here. Did you see him?

ES   I did not pay attention to him. I have a lot of things to think about, as I am running this -

DC   Was this work you set the missing students - to dig the trench - was it done?

ES   No. Unfortunately, as usual, they behave as if they are a law unto themselves.

DC   It is possible, Miss Strutton, that whatever has befallen them had already happened by that time. That it is not their fault.

ES   I don't think anything has *befallen* them. I am sure I am right. I am sorry the police were called in. I did not feel it was necessary but some of the teachers became alarmed, rather foolishly, I have to say.

DC   Their alarm is justified. This is not a part of the country to treat lightly, Miss Strutton. Tell me, what were you doing during the course of today?

ES   Various things.

DC   Be more specific. In writing, with the relevant times. And the same information about the other teachers. From you, Miss Strutton. As quickly as possible. Now, did anything unusual happen yesterday?

ES   No. District Commissioner –

DC   Or in the evening? You said you saw the students at supper.

ES   They were there. I did not pay attention to them, particularly.

DC   So you have no routine for checking on the students during the day or evening?

ES   I am not the police. This is not the way –

DC   Just answer the question, Miss Strutton. It is not a question of policing. I am talking matters of safety and care. This is a wild place, even for those who know it.

ES   As I have said, I have no doubt these children will turn up when it suits them.

DC   I wish I could share your confidence, Miss Strutton. You are aware – I am sure you are, as you have chosen to bring a group of young people to this place - it is possible to live for many days without food, but not without water. It can reach fifty degrees out there on the plains and on exposed faces of the rock. But of course you know this. Let us hope that the local boy, Silowa, is still with them, that they are all together. Silowa, at least, will have the knowledge of where and how to find water, if they are far from Chomlaya's streams. This knowledge, if anything, will save them.

Murothi dropped the papers back on the table. He thought, DC Meshami was made angry by Elisa Strutton. By that peculiar complacency of hers. Is it this woman's ignorance that has produced this disaster?

Suddenly the closeness of wall and roof in the stuffy little room was insufferable; Murothi pushed out, trying to halt the rush of dread and dismay that threatened to cloud his brain.

A sudden breeze lifted the flag, brought the acrid smoke of a charcoal fire, the aroma of maize porridge, the chirp of a child's voice. Life on the compound, after all! Tinny music from a transistor radio floated on the air, and now Murothi spotted the handful of huts behind a sisal hedge at the rear of the compound. Where the families lived, he guessed. A child was peeping through the hedge. At sight of Murothi he ran back, calling. A moment later he emerged, chickens scattering ahead of him, all concentration on carrying a mug without spilling. He handed it up solemnly and scurried back, and Murothi could hear more voices: the woman's and the answering deeper tones of several men.

He sipped the tea, grateful for its hot sweetness, and freshened by the breeze playing swiftly through the yard, humming in the wires of the dog enclosure, rattling dry fronds in the roofs. He watched a man rush from the huts, pulling on the uniform shirt of a constable, saluting Murothi army-style, grinning, hurrying towards the office. And then the child again, in baggy school shorts, cloth bag bouncing on his back, shouting eagerly to other children waiting by the road. Yesterday Murothi had spotted the school on an expanse of dusty grass by the landing strip. Several miles away. An hour's walk: the small green-clad children were running now. It was already hot, and the sun was still low in the sky –

Children missing. *Children*. That is the task. *Children*. And a young woman. Except for Silowa, they knew nothing about this land, could not possibly walk even a mile in such heat without becoming ill. If they had survived till now, how much longer could they? He could not even picture this *Chomlaya* – a long brown snake on the map, high rocks rising from the paler cream of the surrounding terrain.

Nearly three days now since the first alert from the camp at its base. The youngsters could have been gone as much as eight hours by then. Perhaps more! *Nothing* seen of them since, except the miraculous reappearance of Joe, in a place he should not be, a place he almost could not be.

I do not know how the boy could reach the other side of Chomlaya without help, DC Meshami had said. *He could not climb over the ridge – it defies belief. The rocks are ten miles long, in parts very wide across, in parts like a knife edge. Only experienced climbers with ropes and equipment could scale them. It is difficult to travel on foot round the base of the ridge. Our air searches have covered 1,600 square miles, in case these students travelled by vehicle. But we found no vehicle tracks near the north face of the rocks –*

Murothi jumped as, from inside the office, windows were flung open and the telephone rang, shrill and emphatic. Swiftly he drained the last of the tea and, in his room again, sifted through the files and other things taken from the camp by the DC's team. Photos. A large notebook with a red plastic cover decorated with drawings. *The Book Of Days* was printed across the cover. It was the students' camp journal. He had already read it, but he picked it up again and flicked through, stopping at the last entry, the day of the disappearances,

24 February. Nathan (Antelopes).
Stuck in camp. No one gets to move! Anna, Matt, Joe NOWHERE! S is blaming everyone else (surprise surprise). Really BIG argument with B. B wants to call for help on radio — S says he's making a fuss about nothing! B won (for a change). Good thing he came back with the Buffalos from the hot springs, so there's more of us and maybe NOW they'll let us go and look.

Everyone's calling! More later . . .

There wasn't. After that, *The Book Of Days* was blank. There was no mention of the disappearance of Ella's sister.

He turned back a page to the entry on the day before. Different writer.

23 February. Tamara (Buffalos).
We all had to get up in the dark for breakfast at first light and the Buffalos were supposed to be ready to leave for the trip to Lengoi Hot Springs but then Guess Who? got thrown off at the last minute! Miss Strutton picked out Katra and Andy and Phil from the Antelopes to go instead, and they hadn't got packed, so we hung about, played cards, got bored, got more bored, played more cards. When they were ready eventually it was them and the rest of the

Buffalos plus Mr Boyd and Miss Milton and Mr Derby and Tomis, to guide us. Mr Derby's got to help the driver, David, by driving one of the trucks, so I hope he knows what he's doing! It's going to take five or even six hours to get there and it'll be very bumpy because we aren't going on any road and we have to cross the river and there's no bridge or anything so we have to find the right bit or we'll get stuck in the river sand, and we had to pack lots of extra rope and shovels and sacks and planks in case we need them for pulling us out. I'll write all about it when we get back.

There was no record of who had given this to the police. But it must have been a student: this was definitely not for teachers' eyes. Murothi glanced further back through several pages, and a name stopped him. Anna. *The vanished girl.* He hadn't registered the entry before, and was at once annoyed with himself.

He read it now, with extra care.

Second night: bat alert in our tent. The way Candy and Janice shrieked you'd have thought it was an attack by lions. Tomis got it out, and in the morning there were bat droppings all over, poor thing must have been terrified. Then C and J fouled up the stream with a bathload of SHAMPOO AND SOAP. Mr Boyd told them to clear it up. Miss Strutton said it was INTERFERENCE WITH HER

PLAN FOR THE DAY. So the froth sat there drying in the reeds, filthy and grotesque. Mr Boyd was volcanic! He stomped off to do it himself. Charly went to help. So a few of us gave them a hand. Miss Strutton said it was a BREACH OF INSTRUCTIONS and went round with a face like a squashed tomato. She's plotting PUNISHMENTS now. For Mr B too.

Murothi reread it several times. Then he flipped through the pages, looking for any other comments from her. None.

None from Joe or Matt, either.

He was getting a picture of something prickly and unsettled that he had not felt so strongly before. But there was nothing tangible, nothing he could grasp as a direction to follow.

There was another book, black, hardback, written tersely and methodically and always in the same handwriting, called CHOMLAYA LOG. It detailed the members of the Antelopes and Buffalos respectively, their activities and whereabouts each day.

He checked it for the date of The Book Of Days entry by Tamara – 23 Feb:

BUFFALOS

Leaders: Ian Boyd, Helen Milton, Keith Derby.

Departure 0700.

Overnight camp at Lengoi Hot Springs.

Return due 24/2, 16.00.

ANTELOPES

Leaders: Elisa Strutton, Kathleen Hopper, Lawrence Sharp.

Remain at Chomlaya Camp. Writing up last week's activities. Preparations for archaeological field trip and Burukanda Competition.

It was always signed 'ES'. Elisa Strutton. Also presumably the 'S blaming everyone else' mentioned in Nathan's entry who had the 'really big argument with B'. B would be the teacher Ian Boyd. In the Chomlaya Log, Murothi noted, there was no mention of any swapping of people on the Buffalos' trip to Lengoi, or the later-than-planned departure. This was less than accurate, in fact *careless*, from a person who claimed to be so concerned about record-keeping and responsibilities. There was also nothing at all noted in this book on the day of the disappearances itself, 24 February –

Unexpectedly came a glimpse of a trail across the surface of all these other people's words. Urgently, he must find a way to hold it, like setting the plaster cast of a footprint in sand! He shuffled books and folders together, making a quick mental list. First, back to the hospital, speak to Joe. Yesterday, when DC

Meshami tried to question him: *Did you leave together? Did you cross the stream?* not a single question was answered. The boy, it seemed, did not even remember leaving the tents! What could dig such a hole in a youngster's memory?

Next, tackle the DC: if these lost people were to be found – found *in time* – he and DC Meshami must share ideas, not peck and tear at the mystery from rival sides, like vultures –

He stopped. Why did his head bring him these pictures, with their mood of death and decay?

A plan *was* taking shape: suddenly he felt heartened. Rapidly he washed and changed his clothes. Next target: get to Chomlaya. It struck him with the force of sun breaking through cloud that he should take Joe back with him. The sight of Chomlaya again – could this loosen the boy's mind? *If* the boy is well enough, *if* the doctor agrees.

Get the DC's approval. Murothi did not need his permission, but it would be polite, *respectful*, to get his approval.

Finally, he came to thoughts of Ella again – to her small, pale, obstinate face, to her probable terrors at this place, Nanzakoto, which he himself, an African, found strange and alarming enough.

How will I ever be able to tell her, if I have to, that her only sister will never return?

8 a.m.

Ella marched furiously down the corridor. *We are not a hotel!* It wasn't so much the nurse's scalding tongue that upset her; mostly, she was angry at herself. Why did she flee from Joe like that? Squandering the chance to talk to him on her own – probably the only chance she'd get.

Around her, doors banged, water gurgled, half-heard conversations in unknown languages floated down passageways. She reached the end of the corridor and a door held open with buckets of mops and disinfectant bottles. Through it, and she was in a large, paved yard; the clanks and clinks of kitchen work drifted through open windows to one side. Ranks of sheets hung on drying lines and a woman was pegging them out, making a sing-song whistling though her teeth as she moved. She smiled at Ella, bending to her task in a calming rhythmic flow: bend, lift, peg; bend, lift.

This side of the hospital's a better place to wait, Ella thought, looking west towards the mountains: away from sight of the ridges of Chomlaya and the helicopters flying over them.

She stepped out from the shade of the doorway. The air had

lost its moisture. In the fields behind the hospital there was the shimmer of heat – a rippling wrinkle in the bright air – and the rising shrill of insects. The land spread flat and yellow-brown and unchanging until in the far distance it climbed into the mauves and purples of the mountains. From the little plane she'd seen them clearly, fold on delicate fold on the skyline, their peaks circled by pale cloud, their toes deep in forested foothills.

On the other side of those mountains was the border, Inspector Murothi said. Hundreds of miles away. The taxi driver in Ulima said some people believed the vanished foreigners had been kidnapped by soldiers from over there – *that country where terrible, terrible things are happening, just to think of it is enough to make a man lie shivering in his bed.*

Suddenly Ella wanted to run back to the room with Joe, the only person who could say whether Charly's absence was *anything* to do with his own. She couldn't believe they weren't connected, after seeing that photo of them all in the camp. *What'll I do if Joe doesn't remember?* The inspector said the others probably went off for some reason, had an accident, and Charly maybe went looking for them. But alone? Charly? She never took risks that weren't calculated. *Charly* leaving without warning? Telling no one? Not a *single* message?

The sun burned. She could feel it pulsate like a live thing on her shoulders, scorching bare skin at her neck. Sweat trickled below her shirt. She was badly prepared for this, dry-mouthed already. She backed towards the doorway, into shade narrowing with the sharpening angle of the rays.

She was still clutching her sister's letters and emails. She'd told the inspector she had them and he'd asked to see them. But when would he get here? Half past eight at the latest, he'd promised – twenty minutes to go. Then I'll *make* him help me get to Chomlaya. Today. Now.

For perhaps the hundredth time since she'd left London, she unfolded the bundle of papers and lost herself in her sister's words.

From: charlyT@hotmail.com
To: ellaT@hotmail.com
Sent: Tuesday, 14 February, 2006 16:40
Subject: Notes from Chomlaya

Hi Elly! Amazed to get this? Made some good friends in the archaeology camp at Burukanda – offered me use of their internet connection through Ulima Uni. They see me worrying about Little Sister! So, get to use their computer at Burukanda, put stuff on disk – gets emailed from Ulima when they go for supplies. I'll try and write something every few days or so –

letters will be slower - I posted one the day before yesterday.

EMAIL BACK, ELLY, SO I KNOW EVERYTHING'S OK?

Here's the game plan: this first week, mainly getting acclimatised (the heat's ferocious). Some trips along the ridge of Chomlaya + to see the archaeology at Burukanda. Over next 2 weeks there'll be overnight expeditions further afield, and to where we'll be staying to do the labouring work in the 2nd half of the trip. Tomis (he's a ranger here) has been filling me in on the background to it all. Apparently there's serious conflict between herders + their goats and cattle on one hand, and wild animals on the other. They're in competition for the plains - antelope, zebra, buffalo, giraffe etc munch up all-too precious grass, predators threaten people and livestock. So the whole touristy thing with wild animals isn't too popular for people who make a living in the areas (+ Big Money to be made in poaching). Enticing prospect when you're regularly going hungry, as people do here, particularly if the rains fail again. Kasinga (where we're going) is one of the places trying to find an answer. Local community runs tourist things itself for itself, earns income from it, has a stake in conserving animals. That's how it's SUPPOSED to work. In Kasinga they've earned enough to build a small secondary school (two classrooms and an office - there's already a primary school), sink wells, dam part of the river, put in irrigation to nearby fields. Which is where we come in - helping dig foundations for the school and the wells.

Most of the kids are keen, though a few are expending enough energy to sink 10 wells arguing that not everyone should do it + impressively imaginative on alternatives - like a spell on the coast 'researching', no doubt by the sea under palm trees.

So, we'll be spending 10 days hard labour in Kasinga later on, beginning of March (don't know if I'll be able to email from there). Then back at Chomlaya for the final week.

We're SORT OF getting into gear for life in the wild - slowly! Whole day spent sorting out 'toilets'! Digging long trenches, leaving soil piled up behind. When you've used 'toilet', you tip soil over with a spade - the 'flush' system! We dug the 1st trench too close to the stream (Our Leader knew exactly how to do it - she Has Views on Such Matters, even when she's out of her depth, literally! Wouldn't listen to advice from Tomis and Likon - he's the other ranger). Surprise surprise - trench fills with water from below! Had to start again, already tired, got slower and slower, finished too late in dark, still had to erect tents over it. Endless groans from kids (some) and teachers (some) about the labour. Wonder what they thought they'd be doing here?

There was a rumble of wheels, and Ella looked up from her reading. A man trundling a trolley stacked with large metal urns from the kitchen: breakfast for the wards, she guessed. She checked her watch: nearly twenty past eight, Inspector Murothi might be here already –

She stuffed the emails into her pocket and hurried back down the corridor, through the side-door and into the main hospital. And there she halted suddenly, mid-stride, facing a framed newspaper cutting on the wall. 'Minister Opens New Health Centre', was the heading.

She'd seen it last night. The memory brought a sharp flush to her face: on the way to Joe's room, the young nurse, Pirian, scornful, tapping the glass. *Aha! Smart picture, hey? Smart Minister at very smart new hospital. Beautiful new building!*

Startled, Ella had paused, mesmerised by Pirian's emphatic finger, **Tap-tap, tap-tap**: *See here? Aids! Measles! **Tap-tap**. Tuberculosis, malaria, burns, snake bites, buffalo-goring, children crushed by an elephant! We can deal with everything, the Minister says! **Tap-tap**. No problem, he says! We have no money, antibiotics, ointments, vaccines. Of course the Minister of Miracles* *does nothing about this (he is a very busy man). But he leaves us a nice picture to show that he came all the way to Nanzakoto to say there is not another hospital like this for hundreds of miles. Oh yes, we are very much open!*

Now Ella took a deep, steadying breath. All this, yet a region-wide search was needed for four lost tourists! She had a painfully vivid picture of how she must look to Pirian and the other nurses, wandering vacantly round a hospital that had big problems to deal with. How unbearable to spend even one more hour here, useless, and in the way!

Decisively she turned away from the newspaper cutting, dodged past the wards and into the waiting-room.

Already people sat and leaned and lay on every bench, between the benches, against every square of wall; children played in spaces in between. A single, slow ceiling fan barely moved the air. Dust, sweat, and antiseptic-smells mingled, and Ella was assailed by the astonishing scene around her: trousers and dresses, shoes and handbags mingling with spears and sticks and pouches, blanket-cloaks and beaded braids, neckcollars and lip-plugs, armcoils and anklets. People chatted and called to each other, even laughed. Yet in one corner a woman lay on a blanket, listlessly fanned by a child, and an old man stood in the middle, erect and gaunt, one bony foot propped on the other knee, eyes closed, as if he'd remain there, unmoving, for ever.

The buzz of conversation slackened as Ella entered. On all sides eyes turned towards her. Then the room seemed to absorb her existence and the hum resumed. She was alone again, on the edge, with no visible corner to wait in.

She glanced round. No sign of the inspector yet. Through an arch was the clinic treatment area: tables, wash-basins, curtained cubicles, a nurse emerging from one, fetching a bowl, returning. Nearer, a baby lay in the scoop of a weighing machine. Another nurse was busy adjusting the weights, while a young woman watched with such a look on her face that Ella's passing gaze was caught. The baby was silent, moving little. The nurse worked with one hand, propping a small boy on her hip. He was small and thin and naked, and at that moment he writhed fiercely, letting out a yell of such pain, the distress so palpable and frightening that, without thinking, Ella started towards them.

The nurse turned and looked up. It was Pirian.

'If you are idle,' she said, 'you can take the child.'

'I don't know how –'

'He has stomach pain. Bad water. But he is not very ill, and this baby *is*. I must fetch the doctor.' Insistently Pirian held the boy towards Ella. 'He is mainly frightened because his mother is with his sister in the ward. That one is very sick.'

Ella had never held a child before. She was panicked by the wiry strength of him as he arched, pushing away from her, and she nearly dropped him.

'Give him other matters to think about,' Pirian said. 'It will be better for him, and better for me – I can do my work here properly. There is no one else.'

'I –' Ella began, but snapped her mouth shut because Pirian was talking to the young woman, who had lifted her sick baby and was listening with large, still eyes.

The boy twisted again. Ella jiggled him desperately, swung him to her shoulder, pointing at bright magazine pictures tacked to the wall. A brief, hiccupy pause. She moved on, pointed at more pictures. Another sob, but quieter. The tautness of the little body slackened and his head lolled against her shoulder. She rocked him tentatively, seeing Pirian take the woman and baby out of the room, reappear, soap her hands carefully, glancing at Ella as she did so.

'I am sorry for your troubles. For your sister, and for you.' She rinsed and dried her hands, and came to take the boy from Ella. For a second Ella was reluctant to release the small, warm shape snuggling against her. For minutes there had been nothing but the child to think about.

'But you know,' Pirian went on, adjusting the boy against her own shoulder, where he seemed to be asleep, 'people are very strong. Your sister may be very strong. People can endure many surprising things. We see them every day in this place. You should hope – hope is the strongest force there is. Hope gives courage. Truly, I know this.' She went to put the sleeping boy in a cot and Ella followed, working out how to pull up the side and lock it for her. The child lay splayed out in damp exhaustion on the sheet.

'I can stay with him, if you like. I mean, I could help some more till Inspector Murothi comes . . .'

For answer, Pirian only jerked her head towards the waiting-room. 'There is much talk out there. Much, much talk. People tell each other that the English girl should not be so afraid, because Chomlaya is the place of birth, not the place of death. The great rock is the place of life. The place of *life*, you hear me say this? That is the meaning of Chomlaya. It is an old name, of course, but . . .' She did not finish, shrugging slightly and sucking air through her teeth in a soft, thoughtful clicking sound. 'Now, the doctor is seeing your friend, and the policemen have just come. Go now – go, go! You must hear what they say. If you are here later, it will be kind if you will help. We will all still be here.' She grinned wryly and waggled her head. 'We can find many, many things to make you busy! Go!'

Joe eyed the policemen. The two men filled the hospital room. One was short, but broad and powerfully built, in a dark grey uniform. He was doing all the talking. The other, the younger one, did not wear a uniform, and was very tall, stooping slightly as if afraid he would hit his head on the ceiling. Though he said nothing, he seemed to listen carefully, and Joe could feel his eyes on him all the time.

Joe sat on the bed, backed up against the solidity of the frame and the mattress because he felt that everyone here held him responsible, and he didn't know for what.

He wished Ella would come back. Were these the same policemen as yesterday? They'd just told him their names but already everything criss-crossed, tangled, and he was boxed in with questions he couldn't answer, couldn't even hear sometimes, like cotton wool dulled everything outside his head.

'You are a puzzle to us all, young man,' the uniformed one was saying. 'The doctor has just now told us new things. That you are only a little dehydrated. That is rather strange.' He paused here, but getting no response from Joe, resumed, 'You see, Joe – you would be more dehydrated if you were fully exposed to the heat. This suggests to us that you have had shelter, and water, at least for a time. Yet, where you were found over on the north side of the rock is very barren, no shelter there, no vegetation, no water. You see why we are puzzled?'

Silence again, expectant and probing. Joe looked from one to the other. Their anticipation scared him. He cast round desperately for something to say. But the tall one spoke suddenly, his voice quiet and quick in contrast to the deeper, louder tones of the other man. 'It is not to blame you, you understand. District Commissioner Meshami is just hoping that more will come to your memory, to help us.'

'Of course. Inspector Murothi is right,' said the one Joe now knew was the District Commissioner. 'We seek help, not blame.' The man moved to sit down next to Joe, and it was better not having the pair of them drilling into him with their eyes.

'Several puzzles must be solved,' he heard the DC say. 'First, there is how you were wandering around, so far from your camp . . .' He paused, as if to allow this to sink in. 'So, Joe, if you will think again, hard, now that you are more rested. How did you go there? What was your route? It will tell us where to look –'

Joe hesitated. 'I don't know about going anywhere. We were just in the camp. We never went over the rock, we only went to the archaeology dig like everyone else, before, and that's not that way, is it?'

'No, it is not. We can show you a map . . .'

Joe's mind filled with something, like a replay button pushed on.

In the tent. Anna, Silowa, Matt. No light, dark.

Tent. *Charly's* tent. Charly wasn't there.

Something stark and simple penetrated, something he could clear up, that the police had got all wrong. They said Anna, Silowa, Matt and Charly were all missing.

Urgently, he said, 'Wait, wait – Charly just went to the archaeology camp at Burukanda, so she'll be back!'

DC Meshami put out a steadying hand. 'Yes, yes, she went, we know. But she came back the next day, Joe. She was in the camp after you had gone. We *know* this. Did you see her again? Please, please, think.'

He thought. He hung on as hard as he could, dragging the picture out of obscurity. Charly's tent. Flare of moonlight through canvas. Silowa cross-legged on the floor. Anna too. Matt lying on the bed, arguing, 'They'll just find us here, you know they will, Anna. Joe? Joe, won't they just do something else? We've got to tell –'

'Who? Tell who? What's the point!' Anna's voice sharp with insistence. 'Charly's the only one who listens, and *she's* not here. No, we'll *show* them. Joe, Joe – we'll do it, right? Silowa? And after we'll get Charly to –' and Silowa interrupting, 'But I think Matt is right, I think this is very bad things –' and then all stopping, hearing the stealthy brush of movement along the outside of the tent – ●

The memory stalled. Something swung on the edges of his vision, swung and turned, then he had a picture of Anna kneeling, looking down, and a face – *Sean's* face. It appeared suddenly below, and Anna dodged back, out of Sean's sight, shoving Silowa back too –

Then there was just the murk of the tent again and the swing of a black, swaying pendulum –

He pushed hair out of his eyes. His hands were icy but sweaty, as if the thermostat in his body had packed up.

Inspector Murothi caught his eye. It was an alert yet sympathetic glance, and Joe suddenly had the urge to tell him about the nonsensical fragments cluttering his head. But there was a knock on the door, and Ella peered tentatively into the room, seemed to sense she had broken a delicate moment and backed away again.

'Miss Tanner, it is all right,' the DC beckoned her. 'Please stay.' He patted Joe's shoulder. 'These things will return to you, when you are more rested, I think. Do not be disturbed.' He got up. 'For now, Inspector Murothi will be my eyes and ears, and you are to stay with him. Inspector, I will leave you to tell these two young people what will happen now. But I would like a word with you on one or two detailed matters before I leave.'

A quick, reassuring half-smile to Joe from Inspector Murothi. He followed the DC out.

With immense relief, Joe looked at Ella.

Suddenly alone with Joe, every question Ella wanted to ask vanished beneath the temptation to bolt back to the crowded bustle of the clinic. Joe wouldn't want her here, intruding: she turned away, embarrassed, going towards her bag as if she had something to do.

Joe put a hand out to stop her; she felt his fingers hot and tense. 'I was going to come and find you. To ask – things. They said I've been gone for days. Is it true?'

She turned to face him. She said carefully, 'They found you the day before yesterday in the afternoon. Inspector Murothi says you disappeared the day before, maybe quite early in the morning, maybe during the night, even. They don't know, really. So you've been gone maybe a day and half.'

'So the others – it's . . .' He didn't finish.

She filled it in. 'Third day today.'

She saw his shock.

'Charly too?' the question came in a whisper.

This time she didn't answer, just looking at him, helplessly.

After a minute, she said, 'I'm going to make the inspector take me to Chomlaya.'

'Well, you have succeeded!' Inspector Murothi's voice rang from the door. 'We go, all of us, to Chomlaya. We will look for your friends, Joe, and for your sister, Miss Tanner. And we will find them.'

I should not have said that, Murothi thought. I should have been truthful. I should not make promises to these children that I may not be able to keep. I should have said *If they can be found, we will find them.*

'You understand, man,' DC Meshami had told him, 'the temperatures out there are killers. The most urgent thing is to know which direction they took. We need to *focus* our searches.'

'Yes, yes.' Murothi had reassured him. 'These interviews of yours, Sir, they tell a story, but I cannot see it clearly. A two-pronged attack, Sir – your searches continue outside, I will look from *inside*, get to the bottom of things. Sir, I can undertake this for you.'

The DC had appeared to calculate, staring through the window at the encampment of blanket-awnings thrown up by the long-distance travellers waiting their turn in the clinic.

Then, 'Well, we understand each other, Inspector Murothi. I will maintain contact with the British High Commission and the British police. I will tell you as soon as the other parents are contacted. There are unexpected delays – with their children here, they seem to have gone on holiday! But we brace ourselves for their imminent arrival. We are looking for Silowa's people: herders. They move all the time.' He sighed. 'So, now, I will arrange a vehicle to take you to the landing-strip, and you will be flown to Chomlaya. You will receive full cooperation – I have a young sergeant there, Adewa Kaonga, coordinating the continuing investigation. He is intelligent and diligent, and he is aided by two constables, both very good men. They will remain in contact with me and with the team we have assembled with the army on the north side: 24-hour helicopter surveillance, two teams of climbers, with local people who know the terrain . . .'

A pause. Murothi seized it. 'The newspapers speculate

about elephant poachers and cattle raiding . . .'

'Not here. We have active game guards in this region. If the children were caught up in something, we would hear! Inspector Murothi, I have considered whether it may be *kidnap*. Across the border, between the warring rebels and the out-of-control army in that country . . .'

A chill descended on Murothi, contemplating the missing people taken. But emphatically the DC shook his head. 'No, no! No evidence of this – people are not slow to talk. Look, here is what I say to you, my friend: there is enough senseless death and misery in my region. You see it in this hospital! If the rains fail again, there will be desperation. Conflict about access to water will flare up and may reach even here. We are powerless in these matters, men like you and I. But this nonsense of disappearing people – this is something *we* can do. We *will* solve it, yes? If these people are alive, we will bring them back. And if they are not alive, we will learn what has happened.'

For a long moment, DC Meshami had regarded Murothi. 'Truthfully, man, are you sure you wish to take both these children back to Chomlaya camp?'

Murothi was sure: Joe to conjure up obscured memories. Ella – why Ella?

'She has her sister's correspondence. She has knowledge of her sister,' he offered.

But it was not the only truth. It seemed to Murothi that it was the only way to prevent the British High Commission sending Ella back to London. In the remaining camp at Chomlaya, with the other students and teachers and the police presence, she would not be alone while they searched for her sister.

That, Murothi thought, was something *he* could do.

3 p.m.

Leaving the shadow of the helicopter, they step out into the sunlight. A stifling blanket of heat engulfs, and then submerges them, and Ella feels the light as a white pain behind the eyes. It merges with a new, raw fear that is something to do with the vision of Charly lost in this furnace of a place, and something to do with the line of unknown people waiting for them across the expanse of browning plain.

Chomlaya rises a few hundred metres away. Its towering russet walls stretch away to right and left, fringed with green along its base, where Ella knows, from Charly's letter, that the stream runs. In places, foliage drapes its flanks; as they near she can see the hanks and loops of trailing creepers, contours of bushes and trees jutting from ledges and crevices. Between, the rock leans in massive naked slabs or bulges in huge knobbled fists and fingers sculpted by shifting light and shadow so that they seem almost to move against the bleached, painful brilliance of the sky.

In a thicket of green straight ahead are the tents, and to one side an encampment that she can discern as more makeshift, like the one near the hospital, and she guesses it was thrown up by people coming to help with the search.

Then she finds herself wondering, having not thought of this before, if among them is there a father or mother, a sister or brother of Silowa, waiting, hoping, dreading, feeling just as she does.

Murothi has always had feelings about places: calm where contented lives are lived, fear where bad things have happened. He'd sensed that last year where he found the body of the unfortunate murdered tourist – a turmoil in the angry whine of insects along the barren beach that was a remnant of an earlier, bitter quarrel.

Now, he feels Chomlaya. It is a sensation so strong that he slows in his step, and comes to a halt, looking up. As if he is entering the sphere of a vast, quiet, watchful presence. There is no malevolence. Only an overwhelming certainty that everything passing around and over and under it is known, and the rock is unmoved. It is simply there; has always been, will always be, a gigantic rocky spine eroding out of the plain like a beast breaking from the soil. What has it endured? he wonders. What has it survived? And in a fanciful, uncharacteristic way, he finds himself speculating that the rock hears his questions and perceives his profound insignificance against its own unguessable history.

There *must* be stories about it. Snapping back to his policeman's thoughts he senses this may be something missing in the investigation. Stories can move people in unexpected and astonishing ways . . .

He must ask the DC's Sergeant Kaonga. He can see a figure in police uniform leaving the trees and coming towards them, raising a hand in greeting. In response, Murothi raises his own.

And then Joe falters, stumbles, and Murothi reaches to steady him.

The boy is not well, he thinks. I should perhaps not have brought him here; I must pay attention to this too and do what is right, not just what is *useful* . . .

Beneath Joe's feet, the earth tilts; he is awash with sound; tremors pulse through him even as the inspector's grip jolts him back, to here, now, the hot soil beneath his feet, the scratchy bushes, the helicopter behind, the rock, camp, people ahead.

He swallows, and fear is wedged hard between wanting to be back, out there looking for them, to *remember*, and the fog of an unnameable gloom at the emerging tents and people ahead.

Ella slows beside him. Gives him a small, tight smile and keeps steady step with him. *She's scared too, for Charly.*

He gives way to the inspector's hold. Lets him usher them both carefully towards the camp.

Above it all, the rock shimmers: the skitterings and flutterings of myriad insects and lizards, monkeys and birds moving on its ancient cragged face. They ignore the three new animals entering the ring of tents far below. But they look up, restive and wary, as the racing shadow of the eagle spans the cliffs, twists towards the high pinnacles, splinters the air with its harsh, trailing cry – so that even impala and eland far out on the plain raise their heads, and turn towards Chomlaya, and wait.

second day: Chomlaya

daybreak

In the gloom of the tent at first light, alone, Ella found notebook and torch in her pack and wrote,

Well, Charly, I'm here, where you are, and it's just like you said, but also <u>SO</u> different! When we were in the helicopter coming here, Inspector Murothi asked the pilot to fly along the rock, and we followed it winding across the plain like the great big snake you described. I saw how steep and high it is, so I understand why everyone thinks Joe couldn't climb over it. Where they found him it's really just the rocks and dry plain spreading for miles – we flew over that too. There's just one waterhole far out in the middle with herders and cattle milling around a bit of water in a kind of bowl of cracked mud. The pilot said it'll fill up if the rains come next month, and it's the only place that never completely dries because it's fed by some underground source in the volcanic rock below, like the stream along Chomlaya. Then when we got to the camp and I saw all the trees round the camp, I knew why you said you're puzzled why no one lives there – all that water in such a dry place! It is strange, isn't it? The pilot also took us in a big loop over the Burukanda archaeology place – down quite low over the tents and the diggings, and everyone waved at us, and I thought of you going there to email me. I'M SO GLAD I'VE GOT YOUR LETTERS AND EMAILS, CHARLY. I showed them to the inspector. He read them all and asked if he could keep them. But then he looked at me hard, like he knew I need to have them with me, and said he didn't have to take them after all 'but perhaps I can borrow them again later, for a short while, Miss Tanner.' It's odd when he calls me Miss Tanner so I said he didn't need to and now he just says Ella, which is better. When he was reading your letters and emails he showed me where you talk about the 'interesting boy from Burukanda who's friends with some students', and wanted to know if I thought that's Silowa. It is, isn't it? You're friends with Silowa and Matt and Anna, and that's why you're in the photo with them. And maybe you're with them now, but the trouble is we don't know, we can't work anything out, not even if Joe was with you at the beginning. He still doesn't remember anything. And the photo is important, isn't it? I don't know why but I just feel that when I look at it. I told the inspector, and asked him what he thought of that bit in your email about elephants.

She read Charly's email again.

Hi Elly. Here's More Notes from Chomlaya!
Third day, and we've started getting visitors!
Miss S 'disapproves' and instructs us not to

'encourage it'. Haven't figured out yet what she's so knotted up about. The visitors are all children, so curious about what we're doing here. They wander the plains with goats and cattle, v young, v inquisitive, v lively, v keen to show off their English (lucky for me)! There's 4 local languages spoken just round here, 300 in the whole country! The national language is Kisewa, but because English is taught in schools, these children are pretty much fluent – and worth a library of information, I could fill notebooks and notebooks with their chatter! Most of them are from nomadic herder families. There's 3 schools for the whole vast area, and they attend when they're near, when their parents have scraped fees together, when they can be spared from looking after livestock. So by the time they're 14 some have 1 or 2 years at school, others manage a year or 2 more. But they natter on IN ENGLISH about schools, exams, hopes, plans, AMBITIONS. Here's a list: airline pilot, vet, 'environmental' scientist, 'big shot farmer', teacher, to have an enormous herd and get very rich, doctor, rally driver (they've seen the cars going through). They don't have 2p between them, but they don't know the meaning of narrow horizons or limited ambition! It's awful to know the chances of even one of them realising their hopes are so slim as to be almost invisible. They all want pen pals (that's something I CAN DO with some of the students in the camp, and WILL DO when I return, let's do it together, Elly - maybe get your school involved?)

Then one small girl told me her school is closed because of elephants, and I thought she was winding me up! Tomis heard, though, and explained that the elephants have shifted their usual migration route, creating havoc in plantations round several villages. Fences, noise, nothing's turning them away, so they've called in an elephant-diversion-specialist to help sort it out.

I showed him that bit, Charly, Ella carried on writing, because I keep wondering if you've been hurt by animals. We see the vultures in the sky all over, and the animal bones lying in the grass. And Pirian, the nurse in the hospital, said a boy was crushed by an elephant. I can't stop thinking things like that. But the inspector said it isn't likely because we'd find you. Then he got this expression on his face, and looked quickly at Joe too, and sort of hesitated. I think he wished he hadn't started saying that, he meant we'd find your bodies, or maybe your skeletons, so then I wished I hadn't asked, and he said there's no point in wondering about everything that could happen, everyone's got to keep *searching with the helicopters, and we've just got to work out where you've gone. That's why Joe's coming back to Chomlaya, to try and help him remember. It makes him feel really scared that he can't, he looks as if he's hearing things in his head all the time. When we were walking in to the camp I saw he wanted to avoid that teacher – the one you write about. Now I've met her, I see what you mean.*

She remembered: rows of tents like the grid of some gigantic board game; people arrayed like pieces on the board. A handful out in front; knots of others, wary. One or two who offered smiles; not many, most were blank, giving nothing. She remembered the way Miss Strutton marched to overtake the sergeant and reach the inspector first. How she launched into instructions about tents – Joe go to the one he shared with Matt, and Ella to Charly's. Ella hadn't expected this teacher to be small and pretty, or to smile a lot at the inspector, encouragingly, like this was just a friendly visit! She'd kept saying things like, 'I think you'll agree that using *those* tents is by far the most convenient arrangement for everyone. It's really *quite* unnecessary to go to the trouble of putting up *new* tents at this point in time –'

Charly's tent! Spend a night in it – all empty! Just the thought filled Ella with such desolation that she'd struggled to hold back the tears.

I could see the inspector didn't like Miss Strutton's idea. Or her smiles! It all made him angry. He just pretended he didn't hear her. But he stayed very polite and didn't once shout like I half expected him to, when she kept on and on.

So now, we've got a new tent each, Charly. Joe in his and me in mine, both of us right next to the inspector's (but I don't think any of us slept much tonight). I looked outside just now, and saw a torch moving about in Joe's, and there's been a lamp on in the inspector's all night. He's probably reading the interviews again and again – he says funny things like 'we must find the angle of light that will illuminate what we have not seen before' but I know what he means. He says he's going to talk to everyone here _again_, while the army's searches go on. Often I can hear Sergeant Kaonga's voice in the inspector's tent, too, but I don't think anything's happening, there hasn't been any helicopter noise for a bit, though I heard them a while ago. There's two other policemen here as well, keeping contact by radio with the helicopters.

CHARLY, WHERE ARE YOU? HAVEN'T YOU LEFT ME ANY CLUE WHERE YOU'VE GONE? ISN'T THERE ANYTHING TO HELP US?

For a very long while, she sat looking at the last sentences, trying to push back the surge of hopelessness. Make a plan. Make a list of things to do as soon as it's properly light, she told herself. So I don't just wander about and wait, like in the hospital.

In Charly's second letter was her sketch of the rock and the camp and a place over to one side marked with a little stick figure sitting down, and labelled, CHARLY'S PLACE. Below that:

There's this place I go to write up my notes – I really wish you were here to see it, Elly. It's out of the camp, a beach by the stream – fig and tamarind trees lean over it so it's always cool. There's always rustling and scuffling – at first it made me nervous, but then I realised it's just small animals – two tiny antelopes – dik diks – living nearby (Bambis!), frogs and lizards camouflaged so completely you almost never spot them (though I saw a massive green monitor lizard, a metre long or more, I thought it was a crocodile!) – and of course the birds. Even the names are magic – laughing dove, emerald cuckoo, hornbills, sunbirds, hoopoes, golden weavers, purple grenadiers, turacos. High on the rocks are hawk eagles, falcons, red kites, clouds and clouds of swifts and swallows and an eagle owl with a very spooky call, troops of baboons (babies riding their backs) and hundreds of monkeys.

The bigger animals come to drink at the western end of the rock 3 miles away, but we still have to keep a lookout. At night we keep dim lights round the edge of the camp to discourage four-footed visitors. We're circled by glittering eyes — antelope and zebra sneaking in for a closer look. The first night it was really unnerving! It's the weirdest feeling, the way you turn a corner and there's something wild. Dusk yesterday, a pregnant lioness walked across the grass in plain sight of the tents! She stopped, looked at us, we looked at her, then she just went on! Yesterday, our vehicle alarmed a rhino. He galloped at us, changed his mind, head-butted a tree and trotted away with tail up like a flag! There's also our resident leopard — afternoons we've seen him slumped in a tree, flat on his stomach, legs dangling like a sleepy tabby. But then he crossed in front of us one night (the Land Rover was crawling along after dark — we'd got bogged down in sand on the way back from Burukanda, and had to be shunted out by passing herdsmen. They thought the whole thing was very funny!). The leopard was carrying a kill, and he just dropped it and melted away into the dark. We heard him hunting again last night — Likon picked out the rasping cough and made us stop and listen.

Altogether there's something about this place that makes you feel so SMALL. Night's sudden — one minute fiery horizons, next minute deep deep blackness going on forever, you

FEEL the size of the sky! Like it's the beginning of time. We had a storm last night, air suffocating, then lightning like glass breaking, the clouds on fire. Water poured off Chomlaya and boulders smashed down. The camp was a mudbath in minutes. It was just a freak downpour – the rains are weeks away, but it felt as if it could wash us right off the earth!

Abruptly Ella stopped reading. The last words hammered in her head. She could not stand being alone any more. She listened for sounds in the camp. After a minute she located low voices, a swish of footsteps through the grass nearby. She unzipped the tent. Two girls were pouring water from a bucket carried between them, first into a plastic bowl outside the inspector's tent, then Joe's. There was one already left for her.

She took it into her tent, washed, found clean clothes, and suddenly the simple, ordinary tasks gave her a burst of optimism, as if Pirian's words about hope and courage and Chomlaya being the place of life flew into the air around her and lifted her to a brighter place.

I will find you, Charly.

She took the bowl beyond the edge of the camp as she saw others doing, and poured the used water under a thirsty-looking bush. Then she stood looking back at the camp, at how it spread through the trees in the sweeping curve of Chomlaya's precipitous cliffs. On both sides they folded round the cluster of tents, in deep shadow at this hour, for the sun was not yet above the eastern shoulder of the rock. Everything under the trees rippled with green light, leaves and hanging vines rustling in the updraughts of air that constantly stroked the face of the crags. Everywhere, birds alighted daringly on guy ropes or swirled upwards in a glory of crimsons and yellows, purples and greens. Never had Ella heard such a chirruping and warbling, or moved among so many free, wild creatures, so untouchable yet so close; she held tight, in her mind, to Charly's list of magical bird names, to Charly's pleasure at this place, and again she heard her sister's voice, *I wish you were here, Elly, so I could show you . . .*

I am here, Charly. You will.

Then the inspector's voice sounded, calling her and Joe. They all three went together to join Sergeant Kaonga beneath the large white awning furnished with long trestle tables, into the clamour of plates thudding on wood and the hubbub of voices that echoed the moan of search helicopters buzzing on the far side of the rock.

Miss Strutton strode towards them. 'Joe, join that table over there. Inspector, there is a place for you here.'

Ella felt the inspector straighten sharply. 'Thank you, but Joe will stay with me.'

'Inspector, it is inappropriate for Joe not to eat with the other students. He should rejoin the routine of the camp –'

'The boy is here only to assist the police. Otherwise he would be in the hospital. He is not fully well yet, I am sorry to say this, Miss Strutton. It is better that he faces no expectations *except* the return of his memory. I hope *you* will see that it is *appropriate* for this boy to stay in my care. Your routines must go on without him.'

'Inspector, I really don't see . . .'

Ella cast a glance at Joe. He kept his eyes down, refused to look at the woman even when she spoke to him. Except, Ella saw, for a fleeting astonishment when Miss Strutton suddenly stopped arguing and moved away.

'Now the smiling Miss Strutton is not in good humour,' she heard the inspector's murmur to the sergeant. 'It is this way always?'

'Oi, I have seen this!' came the reply. 'If you contradict her too much, she will give you a detention!' The sergeant waggled his head, grinning at his own joke.

Murothi grunted, and Ella noticed how deliberately he turned his back towards Miss Strutton's position at another table. He ushered Ella and Joe to seats, and went off with the sergeant to fetch bowls of food ladled from a large metal pot.

Joe, sitting opposite Ella, was lost at once in some private web of thought. His face was so forlorn, Ella itched to smooth it away.

'Joe?'

He looked up at her.

'You OK?'

As if seeing things for the first time, he looked round, then back at her.

'Bit weird. Sorry – dunno . . .' he spoke hesitantly. But perhaps he looked a little less haunted. Smiled at her even, just slightly.

She concentrated on the bowl of thick, sweet maize porridge the inspector placed in front of her. But hunger warred with a new churning of her stomach at Sergeant Kaonga's morning report to the inspector, delivered rapidly between gulps of tea.

'The climbers have begun again, just now. Yesterday they are going up the gully where Joe was found. They are looking into all the little ravines on the sides. They must go carefully, carefully. Now it is dry, but when the rains come, it runs down this way, angry, angry, everything slips, down, down, sometimes, the rock is just clinging, ready to fall. These people are looking everywhere. Nothing. Today they will go again, straight to the top. This ridge has not been surveyed from close up, on foot. We will hear if they see anything. This is certain. Constable Lesakon and Constable Lakuya will call me on the radio, Sir.'

Ella put her spoon down. The inspector, ever alert, turned to look at her, questioningly.

'There's Charly's place. Like she says in her letter, where she likes to go –'

'Of course, of course,' the sergeant interposed. 'That is not far. Inspector Murothi has already asked of this, and others have told us of your sister's liking for this place. It has been searched. All – from there to there,' he flung his arms to denote the length of the rock. 'It is certain, the whole of the flat area on this side was investigated, on foot and from the helicopters, the first day. Many people came to help! Now it is the turn of the other side.'

'Yes,' Ella said. She picked up the spoon again. She couldn't face even a mouthful. She dropped the spoon into the bowl.

'Eat, Ella,' said the inspector. 'We need you to help us think. The brain needs food. This is our task, to *think*, to ask, to make others think. No despair. The answer is here. The answer *is* here. We will find it.'

Sergeant Kaonga nodded energetically. 'Eat!' he echoed, aiming his words at Joe who was hunched over and staring into space again.

Suddenly two girls at another table stood up, looked round at Joe, and then peered further along where Miss Strutton and the other teachers sat. Joe, with his back to the girls, did not see them.

Rapidly and decisively they crossed the grassy gap between the tables and stopped beside Joe.

'Hey, Joe,' one said. 'How're you doing . . .?' She trailed off at the inadequacy of the question.

As if stung from a daydream, Joe straightened up.

'Where've you been, Joe? I mean, where'd you go? Where's Anna –' stopped by the nudging elbow of the other girl. She reddened, 'Oh, yeah, sorry, only . . . just . . . no one's telling us –'

Joe shook his head, 'It's OK, Tamara – well, it's – sort of . . .'

At which point Tamara seemed to notice something behind Joe. She moved round him sharply and turned her back towards whatever it was. It was such a defiant, blocking gesture, that Ella leaned to see past her at what was there.

Just another group at the next table. Boys and girls. No one looking their way. Nothing in particular Ella could see.

Tamara turned her attention to Ella. 'They say you're Charly's sister? Are you going out on the searches? We're not allowed to. They're afraid we'll get lost. So we're just all hanging about. I'm Tamara, this is Janey. Are we allowed to talk to you? Miss says –'

'Miss doesn't get to say any more,' Joe broke in, abruptly shedding the vagueness. '*He* does,' indicating Inspector Murothi. From his determined concentration on the empty plate in front of him, Ella could tell the policeman was listening to every word.

'Oh, right.' Tamara glanced at Janey as if for guidance. There was none. She went on, 'I s'pose, we've got to go, really. We're on kitchen duty in a minute. We're not doing trips out of the camp, till everyone's found, so Miss's got this B–I–G Idea to get us working on the *Competition*, and she's doing a *Briefing*, at 8.30.' She rolled her eyes elaborately, threw a nervous smile at Joe and Ella, then moved away. Janey followed her a few paces, stopped, turned round again, and said in a rush, aimed at Ella.

'Look, if you – you know – want to hang out, that's our tent over there.' She pointed along the first row. 'Fourth along, the greeny-browny one. Any time, we're just round there all today.'

Surprised, grateful, Ella looked where she pointed, 'Oh! Thanks, if it's OK –'

'Can I say this,' interrupted the inspector, 'you may talk to anybody you wish to, Ella.'

'That's what I said. I'm saying,' Joe muttered with extraordinary ferocity, 'if it's how Miss wants, no one gets to talk to *anyone* about *anything*!'

Janey flashed an embarrassed look at Ella and then Joe. 'Look, Joe, you come over to our tent if you want. There's me and Tamara and Antony and Zak . . . and, you know . . . like, sorry, really . . .' and she marched away rapidly without risk of possible answer, throwing a last, fraught look at Joe.

Light-headed from a night of ragged sleep, Joe watched her go, tensed against the next weird feeling to hit him – flares of colour, tilting ground, like he was on some invisible roller-coaster; or the echo, some bird, twanging his nerves –

Got to work it out. Got to. About Charly, about us being in Charly's tent.

Ask Inspector Murothi. *Can't be the same reason,* Charly being gone. But not in front of Ella. She thinks Charly's with Anna and Matt and Silowa. Don't want her to hear, don't want to make her more scared. Tell her to go with Janey and Tamara, like they said.

Matt. Tent. Matt . . . the struggle to recall, to understand, was a pounding in his head, like trying to batter a door open.

Shadows twisted across the edge of his sight, gone when he tried to look at them. *No*, not shadows, fired with red . . .

Why were we waiting? Why Charly's tent? Why did we GO there, when she wasn't there?

He felt someone stand beside him. Close. He looked up. There, leaning against the table, was Sean.

7 a.m

Sean.

Rewind two weeks. Four days into the trip – Joe's stuttering memory dumps him there all over again.

Breakfast. Matt's on the far side of the table. He's yammering at Anna, peppered with sounds on his harmonica to demonstrate. Joe, sitting opposite, can't really hear, just notes the attentive tilt of Anna's head and likes her for it: Matt rants on a bit about music.

Anna's nodding, offering suggestions. Matt's telling her his new idea – mimicking birdsongs, animal grunts, roars, snuffles. There's been a few in the night, bringing everyone out of bed to the netting at the front of their tents, straining eyes through darkness to spot anything move. Matt stayed up for hours, his shape outlined against the sky as Joe drifted back to sleep.

In the morning he's all charged up about it. 'You can hear a lion's roar five miles away! Tomis told me.' The ranger has been giving them talks: 'Animals of Chomlaya'; Matt fires endless questions, experiments on the harmonica for Tomis's approval. The ranger laughs a lot, entering into the spirit of the enterprise, hooting and snorting and squealing to show Matt.

'Look, look, Joe! Imagine a lion being right up at the tent! Tomis says they come to drink just along the ridge there. And that laughing thing, ending like a groan? That's a hyena, he says they'll sneak right into the camp at night. The snuffly, snorty stuff – that's an anteater. We might get elephants too! Imagine falling into these big holes outside the tent and they're elephant footprints that weren't there when you went to bed. Just *think* what it'd feel like! It's happened to Tomis. He's sleeping near this river, right? The elephants just come round him and drink and then they go away again. He doesn't wake up, just finds it all in the morning!'

'You could do water and wind sounds too,' is Anna's suggestion. 'Let's go along to the stream. There's that place where it gurgles in the rock, and then the swampy, reedy bit with all the rustling. Hey, let's do that later. Joe, what do you think? Matt could call it "Wildsong", or something?'

Joe doesn't know it then, but it's setting her off on some obsession of her own, too. Some time that day she begins the sketching in her logbook. They're all meant to keep a logbook of Chomlaya Camp. But none of them are.

Miss Strutton's spotted that. She's announced a Logbook Inspection. Rewards and Punishments To Follow.

Joe's really thinking about that, half-listening to Matt and Anna. He's deciding: sort something out, quick. Preventative action. Collect stuff – feathers, leaves, seeds – even flakes of bone and flint from the archaeology place. Stick them on the pages, quick. Label them later. *Evasive tactics*. Stop Miss registering his existence.

Third 'inspection' she's called. She's got a thing about inspections. Infusing discipline and team spirit, she calls it. Points given for this, points cancelled for that. *Weird*. Like they're a bunch of primary school kids.

Joe's never been taught by Miss Strutton at school. So, so far he's out of sight, out of mind. Keep it that way, he's thinking. Duck and weave and dodge: bad enough she's got Anna in the line of fire already.

Now Matt's playing rising and falling notes, ending with a fast pulsating sequence: not a bad imitation of one of the birdcalls that echo across the treetops at dusk.

Joe hasn't noticed Sean. No one has. Just, suddenly, that long arm swoops out of nowhere, plucks the harmonica right out of Matt's mouth, and that voice, 'Here, let's *see* that.'

Sean. Joe knows him by sight. He's in the year above at school. Goes round with people Joe knows from swimming club, but he's never spoken to Sean. Nothing to make him stand out, nothing to make him stick in Joe's memory particularly, before.

There is today.

He's turning the harmonica over, looking at it, then he's shoving it in his mouth and blowing. It gives off a kind of strangled screech. A couple of girls nearby laugh, maybe at that, maybe not. But Sean looks at them. Nothing in particular in the look either.

Is there? Maybe there is, in that blankness of his. Like there's no focus in his eyes.

He turns his gaze back to Matt. And then, slowly, to Anna. He looks at her for a moment. A long moment. And she flushes, looks angry. But doesn't say anything, like you'd expect.

And then Sean starts to toss the harmonica. Just a little – throw, catch, throw, catch, throw . . .

'Hey, watch out!' yells Matt, 'you'll drop it, you'll dent it, that's . . .'

Each throw's just a little higher, just a little harder, and Matt, frantic, lunges for it. Sean catches the harmonica above Matt's head, lobs it way out of range, and Matt's leaping to the bench, missing his footing, crashing down, trestles thud over, people topple – squeals, shrieks – Anna trying to pull Matt up, Sean tripping and falling, and the harmonica hits the ground, bounces high on the grass, Matt flinging himself after it, yelling, the uproar sliced by the screech of Miss Strutton's voice.

Not anyone else. *Has* to be Miss Strutton. Like she hovers, somewhere invisible, poised to pounce.

'Anna! *Again!*'

And Matt's shout, 'No, Miss! It's him, he's nicked my harmonica!'

'No, I have it, and it's *mine* now. *Permanently.* If your minuscule brain can absorb such a word.' She rakes them with her practised look of distaste. 'If you two think you can run amok whenever you like, you can think again. No trips – for either of you – today. Clear up round camp. On second thoughts, you can also do the meals today. *All* of them. Report to me this evening.' She ignores Matt's, 'But Miss, he just swiped it . . .' and Anna's open stare of contempt.

'Now, Sean, go and help Katra get the solar shower up into the tree. *That* genius girl has just designed one. Worth a few team points between you, I'd say, to make up for the ones *other* people work so *hard* at losing. *Won't it?*'

Miss Strutton.

Miss Strutton and her team points. Miss Strutton and Sean.

Miss Strutton and her aren't-they-always-right, aren't-they-

always-brilliant little helpers.

Sean was still there, Ella still opposite on the far side of the table, the inspector still beside her. As if the moment was frozen in time.

Without looking towards him, Joe could sense the policeman's watchful gaze.

Sean, though, was doing nothing, just lolling against the table, hands stuffed deep in his pockets. He was surveying Joe. Then he turned his attention to Ella. It was the way Joe remembered him looking at Anna that day. Up and down. This time Sean gave Ella a wide, white-toothed smile. Ella looked away, startled and embarrassed by the scrutiny.

Joe wanted to hit Sean, knock him back, felt his own face blanch with the rush and rage of it.

No. He steadied himself. *Just let Sean hear you tell the inspector . . .*

Wrong. Opens the field to when the inspector isn't here. Invites Sean back some other time.

He caught the inspector's eye; could tell he was reading this.

He skimmed his gaze past Sean. *Don't see you, don't know you're there, don't see you at all.*

And walked away. No looking at Ella, no drawing fire towards her. No glancing back. With every ounce of self-control he wanted to hide from Sean that he'd even noticed he was there.

Murothi observed the encounter in all its detail. He noted the clench-jawed willpower of Joe's exit, and then the flutter of disturbance in the other's face. Surprise?

He took in other things too, storing them like an inventory. The boy's looks: unusually tall, well-built, black-haired, wild, messed-up hair, the tips dyed fair. Time had been spent on this hairstyle. Most of the other students, particularly the boys, had the ragged look you would expect in youngsters unused to anything but city lives with ample running water and clean clothes provided. A few were enjoying a lengthy holiday from serious washing.

Not this boy. Everything designed, scrupulously planned: the round-shouldered nonchalance, the mannered slouch as he turned his back on the departing Joe and gave Ella another deliberate, appraising look, rudely obvious to the policemen.

The boy strolled away. He passed close behind Sergeant Kaonga but without so much as a glance at either policeman.

Murothi leaned towards the sergeant. 'You know this one?'

'Miss Strutton speaks of him often, Sir. Sean *this*, Sean *that*! We hear this name many times. But I have not heard of a *connection* with our missing ones.'

'He was trying to frighten Joe,' said Ella. 'But Joe was just angry.'

Murothi regarded her thoughtfully. 'Ah, you have seen it, Ella. Yes . . .'

The sergeant turned his mug of tea in his hands, staring into it as if for inspiration, then up at Murothi again. 'I *have* seen that his friends are those.' He tipped his head towards a group visible to Ella and Murothi over the sergeant's shoulder.

Rapidly, Murothi scanned the seated students and made a mental note of two girls, two boys, who, it struck him, were very much aware of his glance and of Ella beside him. They were now paying particular attention to Sean's departure.

'Let me say this,' Sergeant Kaonga mused, 'I have heard of this from my friend Samuel Lekitumu. This is the man I have told you about, Sir, the cook for this camp. This is very lucky for us! He has been here since these people made this camp at Chomlaya. Samuel is my old, old friend – from school we have known each other. I have spoken to him much. Samuel tells me that this Miss Strutton has friends, like this Sean and *his* friends. And then there are all the other people who do not matter to her. Teachers, students, she divides them all up like this. In little boxes, she locks them in! *That one* agrees with me, so that one is my friend. *That one* does not agree with me so that one is not my friend. In fact, that one is going to be my enemy.' He wrinkled his nose, as if the whole thought produced a stench. 'I have thought that when this teacher is discontented, somebody will suffer. Here, it will be a child who will suffer, I think so. I will ask Samuel Lekitumu more of this Sean person, but,' he shook his head, 'these matters have nothing to do with our missing ones. I think nothing . . .'

'Yes, and no. No and yes, perhaps. Has Samuel told you that Miss Strutton *has* been discontented here?'

'There's what Charly says,' Ella interrupted, listening curiously to all of this. 'Inspector, you saw what she wrote about Miss Strutton.'

'She does, you are right. Sergeant?'

Sergeant Kaonga considered the question. 'The teacher Ian Boyd and Miss Strutton do not agree on many things,' he commented slowly. 'I have heard him argue with her. It is the one sitting there.' Again he made a movement of his head, a jutting of the chin, this time towards where the teachers had been breakfasting. The table was empty now of all but one man. At once he seemed conscious of the policemen's gaze, standing up as if to come over to them.

'Hoi!' the sergeant warned Murothi. 'She advances!'

Ian Boyd looked towards Miss Strutton, Ella saw, appeared to change his mind, and walked away.

Miss Strutton was nearing fast, chatting to students, to another teacher – who nodded and went hurrying away – to more students.

'She wishes us to see her review her troops, I think,' the sergeant muttered to the inspector. 'She is a Big-Chief General, I think, in her head.'

'Well, everyone,' Miss Strutton said, very brightly, arriving, but ignoring the sergeant and Ella, her attention only on the inspector: 'so what does the rest of today bring?'

She's nervous! Ella thought. She marches off before, all angry, and now she's back already, because she can't stand not knowing what the inspector's going to do!

'The search continues, Miss Strutton, obviously,' the inspector replied. 'Climbers and helicopters are out now. Meanwhile I will speak to everyone –'

'Who? We've all been interviewed already!' Miss Strutton stopped, lightened her tone, enlarged her smile, and went on, 'The thing is, you may not have been told, of course, but you should *understand* that these missing students were consistently disobedient, always in trouble . . . the truth is, they have simply ignored the rules, and stupidly got themselves lost.'

'Let us hope and pray fervently, then, Miss Strutton, that they will *return* and get the opportunity to be disobedient again, and you will have the task of disciplining them. For whatever misbehaviour you are so certain they have committed. It is an outcome to be hoped for, I think?'

The smile slid right off Miss Strutton's face.

The sergeant exchanged a look with Ella, imperceptibly raising one eyebrow before recomposing his face in an expression of polite attention. Ella had difficulty suppressing a giggle.

The inspector pressed, 'Perhaps you will explain to me the rules about leaving the camp? The ones you feel these students have disobeyed?'

'I've already –'

'I would like to hear it again, you see, because today is a new day, and with a new day, new light always shines. Things may reveal themselves that were obscure yesterday. *Today* we have the significant benefit of Joe's return. We must leave no stone unturned. Go through it again, Miss Strutton. Quickly. This is already taking too much time.'

Her lips compressed thinly. 'The rules are very clear. Not to leave the area of the camp except with an adult. The perimeter of free movement for the students, without supervision by an adult, is explicitly defined.'

'And that is?'

Now the teacher's voice was shrill with irritation. 'The flat area only, and the path up the cliff – no climbing on the rocks at all, anywhere. Only as far as particular landmarks. Only to where the path finishes that way, for example,' she flapped a hand towards the leaning buttress of rock to the east.

'And the other way?'

She sighed testily.

The sergeant offered, 'I will show you, Sir –'

'With all due respect, as I have repeatedly said,' the teacher interrupted frostily, 'this is all of no importance, you see. The *rules* are of no importance, as these particular students always looked for ways of breaking them.'

'Is this really true?' the inspector asked.

Disbelief froze the expression on her face. 'The truth is, Anna should not have been allowed to come on this expedition to Africa at all, Inspector,' she snapped. 'She is not a suitable candidate for this kind of experience. She goes her own sweet way, regardless, and drags others with her. I opposed her coming, but Mr Boyd persuaded the head teacher. Regrettable.

A recipe for trouble. And now we have trouble.' She ended, to Ella's utter astonishment, with a smile of satisfaction.

'And *I* ask again, Miss Strutton, is this really true? There is the African boy, Silowa, to consider. And the journalist, Charlotte Tanner. I do not see how disobedience of your camp rules for students is relevant to them.'

Ella saw that the teacher's face was no longer in the slightest bit pretty, but sour and unpleasant as if it had never softened into even a whisper of a smile. Her gaze was now drifting into the middle distance where apparently she saw something that claimed instant attention. She muttered something inaudible and went.

The sergeant gave the inspector a beam of pure, undisguised satisfaction. 'Of course, when the DC was here, she tried to be *very* polite.'

The inspector, however, was visibly annoyed with himself. 'Why do we waste precious time arguing with this person? She will put us in this big box of enemies. We should arrest her for obstruction!'

'Ah, Sir! The Minister would not like it. It would not look good in the newspaper,' countered the sergeant mischievously.

'Well,' Inspector Murothi got up decisively, 'Sergeant, show me these places the students could go. That is the first task. We take Joe, we visit them together –'

'And me!' Ella jumped in. 'Inspector, *please*!'

'Ah, Ella, I am sorry, it would be better to join those two girls who invited you. I do not want –'

She knew it: he was thinking *in case we find something bad.* 'But I can't just hang about waiting!'

'Sir, these places are *well* searched already,' put in the sergeant, with emphasis and a meaningful look at the inspector.

The inspector looked from the sergeant back to Ella. After a minute, he sighed, with a rueful smile. 'OK, OK. You win! You are a determined young woman, I see, and you have recruited Sergeant Kaonga to your cause! So, we will go, all of us. To help Joe remember.'

'And Tomis or Likon too. They know this Chomlaya like it is their own hand! They will be good help. I will find one of them. We depart now, before the heat is up.' The sergeant hurried off.

'I'll get water for us all, and hats.' Ella rushed away too, to prove her usefulness before the inspector could change his mind.

It is important, Murothi was thinking, turning to go in search of Joe, to gain the boy's confidence. Not to confront him too fiercely or he will retreat again. In the hours before sleep last night, Murothi had tried several conversations; each had ended with the terrible blank fright in Joe's face.

Ella, Murothi thought now, can help with this. Whenever he is most unhappy, the boy draws towards Ella. He will speak to her when he cannot speak to me. Perhaps. She has a measure of his mood.

The camp troubles him, I see this, too.

Something here I did not expect. Strains. Quarrels. Rifts between one student and another. This is all *inside* the camp, not *outside*, and *I had not seen that*. A prickle of coldness passed over him. Has harm been done to these children from *within*? Are they more than just lost?

Ella, heading towards the kitchen area in search of water, stepped over guy ropes between the tents, and saw the way was blocked.

She turned round; the way was blocked again. A girl in front and a girl behind. Casual, but in the way.

Before she could squeeze by, the one behind said, 'Hey, you – whatever your name is. What's going on?'

Startled, Ella looked back at her. 'Sorry?'

'I *said*,' the tone was impatient, sharp, 'what's –'

But she didn't finish, shoving past with such violence that

Ella was flung sideways over a guy rope, tripping on a tent peg and stabbing her ankle.

'Later,' hissed the girl, and yanked her friend away.

Ella looked round. No one else in sight. It dawned on her that these two were the ones the sergeant said were Sean's friends. Warily, she picked her way across the remaining ropes, and only then registered the man ahead, paused with his arms full of wood, watching.

Those girls saw him. It's what scared them off.

The man was making a show of observing them till they were out of sight. Then he shook his head and returned to stoking the fire in a large half oil drum tipped on its side. Satisfied, he balanced a grille across the top, lifted several pots from the ground and placed them to heat.

Now he looked up at Ella coming towards him, greeting her with a wide smile.

She said, 'Excuse me, I'm –'

'The sister of Charly,' he acknowledged. 'I know this. And I am Samuel Lekitumu, feeder of multitudes! And I must give my instructions.' He indicated students behind him, carrying things from a tent to trestle tables ranged on one side of the working area. 'I will return!' He moved away, organising two people to sort utensils, another to scoop beans from a sack into a large flat pan. Others, kneeling by the stream, were washing up in plastic bowls, talking loudly, stacking things to dry on grilles propped between stones. One saw Ella and waved. It was Tamara, and the ordinary friendliness of the greeting quelled the last of Ella's unease at the peculiar incident with the other two girls.

'Do I get drinking water here or from the stream?' she asked Samuel as soon as he returned. 'It's to take with us. I mean for the policemen and me and Joe.'

Samuel pointed to water bottles dangling by straps from a tree branch, and a metal tank standing below it. A ladle hung on a twig.

'Take, please,' he said. 'It is good and fresh. The students fetch it from the stream, high up, where it escapes from the rock.' He pointed, and she saw the telltale line of a moist gully and lush green foliage that marked water springing from a cleft in the cliff. She went over and took a water bottle from the twig.

'It is better if you take one for each person,' suggested Samuel.

She unhooked five bottles, then added a sixth, just in case. She ladled water into them, conscious of the wasteful spill on the ground.

Politely Samuel paid no attention. He stoked the fire with more wood, large and calm and deliberate in his movements, saying, after a moment, 'Miss Charly's Sister, let me say this to you: these girls – the ones who stop you there – do not let them trouble you. They are small people. They wish to play big games. But they cannot truly hurt people who have good hearts.'

'Yes, but I don't know what they wanted,' replied Ella, relieved to talk about it.

There was silence; she could see Samuel was thinking. She filled another bottle.

Finally he said, 'There are some who think that if young people have to look for firewood and carry water when it is not their accustomed life, like magic they will have great knowledge of things beyond them! These people do not see that to understand somebody, you must go with them on a journey!' He sniffed, disparaging.

Ella hadn't the faintest idea what he meant. As if reading her mind, Samuel went on, 'But this is what I say to you. Your sister is not so foolish. Charly has respect for Chomlaya. This will keep her safe. Daylight always follows a dark night – there will be this dawn. They will return: Chomlaya will return them.'

Ella could not answer. Other possibilities, terrible possibilities, submerged her. She concentrated very hard on filling the last bottle, screwing on the cap, hanging the ladle back on its twig.

He watched her, and then came over, turning her to face him, his hands solid and warm on her shoulders. 'Listen to me, little sister of Charly. Your sister is a person with great curiosity. We have many talks, many times – *she* is a listener, your sister. She *hears*. She is interested that I work for the field camps of the archaeology expeditions, she asks to know about the places I go and the people I feed! She knows that the stomach makes good friends! Yes,' he laughed lightly, 'we speak many times. I know this sister of yours. She will be back, you see, to ask more questions!' He nodded. 'She will.' He bent down and began to gather the bottles for her.

At that moment, from behind the store tent, a man appeared, striding purposefully towards Samuel. In her letter, Charly had talked of the *sinewy height and strength of the herders – honed by vast distances roamed with their livestock.* This man was one of them, Ella saw at once. He was different again from the people she'd seen in the hospital: hair braided into a gleaming crest across his scalp; long wood plugs heavy in his ears; red blanket cloak tied at the shoulder. He carried a leather pouch and a heavy stick, sharpened to a lethal point, which he swung on to his shoulder and rested there.

He greeted Samuel, giving Ella a long, considering look. He and Samuel spoke rapidly and Samuel turned to her. 'This is

Mungai, the cousin of the boy Silowa, who is lost. Mungai has been passing many days to the north with the cattle, and has only just heard of Silowa's trouble. I have told him of your sister. He is telling you of his sympathy. He has no English.'

Ella said, 'I'm sorry about Silowa too . . .'

'Offer your hand as you say this,' said Samuel. 'He will approve of your courtesy.'

Ella did so. Mungai shook it, listening carefully while Samuel translated her words.

'He is upset that Silowa has run from his family to the archaeology place at Burukanda,' Samuel explained, waving his hand towards the plains. 'He thinks it is a foolish thing, and that this trouble of Silowa's has come from it.'

In a rush, Ella said, 'Say the inspector is sure we'll find them. We're going out now to help Joe remember where they went,' and at once Samuel translated for her.

At this, Mungai reached out and took both her hands, holding them firmly, answering with enthusiasm.

'He is wishing you and your sister very well,' Samuel told her, 'and he says –'

'*Ella!*' Miss Strutton's unmistakable voice rang across the clearing. 'I would appreciate it if you would remember that I have rules about random outsiders wandering about my camp.'

Her meaning, her *rudeness* hit Ella with the punch of a physical blow. 'It's Silowa's cousin!' she retorted. She could feel Samuel's anger like a palpable heat off his skin, how he drew himself to his full bear-like height.

Mungai made some remark to Samuel, offered his hand again to them both. Without so much as a glance towards the teacher marching across the clearing, he turned his back on her and walked away.

'He will talk to the policemen,' Samuel informed Ella. 'You should make sure Inspector Murothi and Sergeant Kaonga know that he is here.'

Ella could feel Miss Strutton looking from one to the other, expecting them to speak to her. But Samuel just handed Ella the water bottles and turned away to poke the fire, and Ella checked all the caps were tight, gathered the straps together and heaved them over her shoulder.

'Ella! There you are,' cried the sergeant, emerging from between the nearest tents with the inspector and Joe. 'And Samuel! Inspector Murothi, this is my good friend Samuel Lekitumu, as I have told you.'

Miss Strutton's face took on a look of pinched fury. She stalked her way to the students washing up by the stream, gave some order that sent two of them running off and reduced the others to silence, looking down.

Samuel shook the inspector's hand and sucked air through his teeth, clicking his tongue. 'She watches the pot all the time,' he said, 'but she never makes the stew, that one. But you can be sure she will always eat it.' He looked meaningfully at the inspector, peered into the pots on the fire, and stirred one.

'Samuel has a picture for everything,' remarked Sergeant Kaonga. 'You must leave a day for every conversation. And another day to work out what he means.'

'An old goat does not sneeze for nothing,' retorted Samuel. He adjusted the straps of the water bottles more comfortably on Ella's shoulder.

'Hoi, we will be back to hear more.' The sergeant clapped him on the arm and began to usher the group towards the path along the stream.

'Remember,' answered Samuel, 'when the crocodile smiles, be extra careful.' He was watching Miss Strutton, who had stopped within view.

She was talking to Sean. And Ella noticed that she was laughing.

8 a.m

The narrow track through tall grasses hugged the stream along the snaking curves of the ridge to the west. The column moved in single file, Sergeant Kaonga leading, then the inspector, Joe, Ella, and lastly Tomis, the ranger falling into step behind her in an easy, loose-limbed stroll and giving Ella a welcome feeling of protection.

But the walk was unnerving her. Joe kept looking round, as if expecting something to appear on the path. And pausing, as if listening. The inspector and the sergeant seemed to note every glance and pause, but they asked no questions. Talking to Samuel, Ella had built this expedition in her mind into the key that would unlock something for Joe; somewhere along here, he would reveal everything and they could all go racing to the rescue.

Instead they moved steadily further from the camp and away from the rumble of helicopters beyond the cliffs. And still Joe said nothing; a kind of silence fell on them all in the wake of his silence. No one dared to break it.

Tiny beaches of soft sand cut across their route. Low bushes rattled to the scuttle of small animals. They wound through reeds, zigzagged between boulders, skirted wide round dark copses of trees and curtaining creepers, and emerged a half-mile along, on to a plateau of rock – large slabs sloping in smooth, flat steps down from the base of the cliff. Here the stream pooled below the blue shimmer of dragonflies, and shrill screams of alarm rang from a horde of frantic brown shapes skittering away from Ella's feet.

Tomis caught her, steadying. 'Rock hyrax. They will not harm. They will watch us up there and be angry that we invade their place!' He pointed and Ella looked, but could see nothing against the dark bulk of Chomlaya, only massed shadows and leaning summits, and above it all, the high white gleam of sky.

Now the path crossed the water towards the cliff. It took them on to rock greened and slippery with lichens and mosses; then over higher slabs, where they picked their way through fresh animal spoor scattered on the pocked, ridged surfaces. The droppings were still hot, reeking and steaming in the warmth. 'A very small antelope,' Tomis informed her softly. 'A klipspringer. It likes the rocks. It is now hiding above us, close by, and peeping at us.' And a few steps further on he tapped her arm to alert her to other presences in the thinner woodland spreading to their left towards the plain: buffalo ambling among the trees, silhouettes against the paler grasses beyond; the tell-tale twitching of antelope flicking their tails. 'Gazelle, impala, a few waterbuck, too.'

His whispers interrupted her increasingly anxious scrutiny of foliage and rocks, and she was grateful. It had all been searched before, and then searched again and again. But she couldn't help hoping that her eye would catch an out-of-place colour or jerk of movement.

Beyond the rocky plateau, the path split into two tracks. One held close to the base of Chomlaya onward into a marshy stretch of giant rushes bordered by yellow-trunked fever trees. The other track folded back in the direction they had come from, and rose steeply to a broad ledge against the cliffs. At the lower levels it was thickly canopied by stunted trees, so that the path seemed to enter a luminous green tunnel. Above, jagged rock stabbed upwards, thronged with big, dark, raucous birds swirling away from the crags like storm clouds boiling against the sky.

Sergeant Kaonga had stopped where the tracks divided. All except Tomis were panting with the intensifying heat and the exertion of climbing. Ella lifted the water bottle on its strap round her neck, and drank deeply. Tomis took hold of Joe's, unscrewed the cap, handed it to him, instructing him to drink in short, frequent sips.

'This is as far as anyone from the camp may go in that direction.' The sergeant indicated the lower path straight on through the rushes. 'That leads on to the drinking place where many, many big animals are gathering. We do not go closer! *That* way,' indicating the path curling upward through the leafy tunnel, 'goes high on the rocks. I am told people from the camp were allowed to go up there if they stayed in groups of at least four. When you get along a little way, you can see the camp from above –'

The inspector put a hand on his arm, silencing him: Joe was moving up this track. Instantly, they fell into step behind.

The path, bound by gnarled tree roots eroding out of the stony soil, was broad and easy to walk. But the drop to Ella's right, glimpsed now and then through the mesh of twisted tree trunks, was increasingly sheer, and the thick foliage arching above her head quivered with the unseen antics of monkeys. Hearing their chittering, chattering commentary, she was suddenly afraid. Joe was now moving fast, and she had the terrifying premonition that he had remembered something, that the monkeys knew it and were leading them there, that beyond this green tunnel, something would be waiting for them. Her heart raced and her mind filled with a blanking panic; she jumped involuntarily at a swinging tail whipping past her head and a small, bright-eyed face, poised, peering curiously, and then as suddenly gone.

But the track simply left the tunnelled gloom of the trees, and the camp tents were in view, far below, coming and going through the feathery acacia branches of the lower woods. There was nothing else to see; she was being stupid. Joe had halted and was just looking down at the camp.

She stood beside him. At once she recognised the view. 'Charly's map! She was here when she did it, wasn't she?' She pulled the letter from her pocket, showed him. He took it and nodded; he looked right and left along the ridge, watched the speck of a helicopter against the flare of the sun.

'The clearest view is from here.' Sergeant Kaonga was standing where the stony track broadened into a round platform of rock. 'There – you see all the camp. This path goes on a little more, but stops just there –'

'No, it doesn't stop. Just *looks* like it,' broke in Joe. Since that waking moment in the hospital, this scene endlessly replayed in his head. Anna, Matt, Silowa, himself, climbing . . . 'We went up there – *right* up,' he said.

Gigantic boulders crowned the crags in precarious knobbly formations. In one place the lip of the cliff had split, toppling boulders into a narrow cleft in the otherwise unbroken line of the heights. From this angle they could see how the cleft deepened and broadened into a plunging ravine flanked by walls of reddish rock seamed in multicoloured streaks – like ribs rippled by the play of birds across them.

'Up top, it's Silowa's lookout place,' Joe said. 'There was this time Silowa got sent back from here . . .' he trailed off, looking around him.

'And?' Ella urged him.

For a moment he gazed at her, as if not seeing her, as if he was thinking hard. Then he turned to Tomis. 'That time – remember?'

Tomis frowned. Squatting on his heels at the edge of the rock he had been scrutinising the slopes below them. Then his face cleared. 'It is true! In all these times and all these places we go to, I forget. Yes, it is in the first days here. Everyone climbs to this place. But then – trouble, trouble, trouble!' He clucked his tongue. 'The expedition begins late – already it is too hot. But the teachers, they think about other things, they do not check properly. We tell them, but they do not check! Some students – no water. We must share bottles and send people back to refill from the stream. Some – no hats. Some – blisters. One, very, very bad blisters – bleeding. *Everyone* bad-tempered from the heat. Some get sick. One boy is stung –'

'And Anna was talking to Silowa,' Joe interrupted, 'and Miss Strutton said they were slowing us down, trailing at the back, Silowa shouldn't be hanging around us, you know the way she says! She told him to go, she told Anna to go back to camp. You said no, and then Mr Boyd came –'

'No one should walk this path alone,' emphatically Tomis agreed. 'Always there is risk of snakes and animals. But Miss Strutton of course is in charge! This time, Ian argues with her, but Silowa – oh! He is very upset. He runs away! Anna wishes to fetch him, but Ian insists she must stay with the group. The mood is bad, very bad! But everyone continues to where the path stops. It is –' he made a chopping movement with his hand, 'steep there. Filled up with fallen rocks and trees. Only a monkey can pass that way.'

'No, like I said, it *looks* like the path stops,' Joe insisted vehemently, 'but you go *under*. There's bushes all over so you don't notice. You can crawl right through the rocks and then you get on to the top. Silowa was going to show everyone, but instead he just brought Anna and me and Matt back. Later . . .'

He sees it; as if they're with him again. Silowa's bare feet padding between boulders; dust puffs from his heels. He looks

back, beckons, and Anna races past him, *Hey, Joe, up here!
Here! Oh, wow! I could stay here forever. I could build a house and
live here forever! Silowa, your place is the best, best in the world!*

Tip-toe on a turret of rock, Silowa's laughing – hand on
Joe's shoulder, hand on Anna's, balanced between them. *It is
ours, now, yes? I show it to you, and we share it! Matt, Matt! I
come too,* he yells at Matt clambering higher, slithering back,
finally triumphant, poised like a piper with an invisible pipe,
drawing the eagle up from the ravine, dark wings soaring
through glowing air. *My friend Ndigi will make you a pipe, Matt!
I will ask him. I will bring it to you, yes? My friend will be happy to
do this! He is a musician, like you, he plays as he wanders . . .*
sweeping his arm wide . . . *we see to the beginning of time!* and Joe
remembers how even the giraffe far below in their undulating
walk against the blood-red sky look like primeval creatures
stalking the setting sun.

He remembers wanting to trap the moment forever. Even
just with a photo –

But Miss had my camera, he thought savagely.

He saw the inspector watching him carefully. 'Is this where
you came with your friends?' he heard his voice. 'Should we
search again here?'

'No, I mean, we came here plenty of times at first,' said Joe.

'But other places, too, after. I'd have photos, but Miss Strutton took my camera –'

'Your camera? Why does she do this?' The inspector's voice was sharp, alert, and Ella, who had been gazing down at the camp as she listened, looked up quickly, as if expecting something important.

'It's nothing,' Joe explained hurriedly, 'really, it's nothing, I mean, I was just taking pictures in the camp and she was having this argument with Mr Boyd, wasn't she? Yelling – really mad! She thought I'd taken a picture, why would I want a picture of her? So she confiscated the camera. That's the way she is. Won't listen.'

There was a pause, and this time the inspector broke it softly. 'And now that you recall this place, Joe, is there more you can remember?'

'This isn't stuff I forgot – it's all *before*.'

'Before what?'

A longer silence. Ella held her breath.

'Before what I already told you,' Joe said. 'In Charly's tent –'

'And do you remember now why you went to Charly's tent?'

The inspector's voice blurred. Joe couldn't draw breath, his tongue thickening. He swallowed hard, tried to fight it off, looked away, helpless.

Ella saw Joe snapping back into himself, and the barely masked frustration flare on the inspector's face. Her own throat suddenly rasped with thirst; a persistent drumming filled her head.

By her watch it was only forty minutes since they'd left the camp. She pulled her hat lower against the intensifying glare. The rays of the climbing sun had just tipped across the eastern rim of Chomlaya, and second by second, light poured down the crags above them like an advancing tide carrying despair with it. They had climbed because Joe remembered this climb. But it was a false hope. It wasn't telling them where Charly or Matt or Anna or Silowa were; the distant moan of the helicopters sent an unrelenting reminder. Now and then they rose into view, making steep banking turns as if something new was happening. But it wasn't.

'So, we will visit this path of Silowa's: Tomis and I,' Sergeant Kaonga announced briskly, and the two of them moved off.

At his voice, Joe gave a start and turned to follow. Swiftly the inspector intervened, 'No, no, I think we will sit, Joe. You too, Ella. We will drink some more, and tired Murothi will have a rest.'

Tomis and the sergeant were nearing the rim of the ravine. Ella saw them stop, and turn, and survey the vast slabs of rock rising sheer from the path. Then both men stepped closer and pulled bushes and creepers aside. Sergeant Kaonga bent double. He appeared to melt into the rocks, Tomis too, and suddenly their voices could be heard, floating from somewhere beyond view.

Joe, observing it all intently, seemed suddenly to lighten. His face cleared, and he became aware of Ella's gaze. He looked properly at her, not through her as if she wasn't there.

'Charly went up there with us, one time,' he offered.

'Rest, now,' the inspector, cross-legged, drinking from his water bottle, patted the rock beside him. 'Rest properly. Sit. And now, Joe, you can tell us more about this interesting boy, Silowa? How you came to know him?'

How? Silowa *found* us, Joe thought. There was just the Buffalos at Burukanda, and Véronique, the archaeologist, and her 'Introduction to Archaeology' talk. One minute we don't know Silowa, next minute he's there . . .

Imagine, Joe remembers Véronique saying. *Imagine that all this — this vast wilderness — is an enormous lake . . .*

Actually they're standing on stony earth. No water anywhere. Endless whiteness all round – not even the skeleton of a thornbush. It's a shallow gully. Further along it cuts deeper, twists through rocks sticking up from the sand like swollen knuckles.

Cast your mind back to one and a half million years ago, Véronique is saying.

Everyone's listening to her, pretty much. Not Janice and Candy, though – whining, working hard at boredom, flopped on the ground, furiously fanning their hats, demanding loudly what's happening next. Worse than usual. Worse since they've started hanging out with Sean in the camp. Worse since that row about them messing up the stream.

Mr Boyd would've squashed the whining flat. But he's not here, and the others, Mr Sharp and Miss Hopper, they're too busy yakking to each other, and now they've disappeared to sit in the shade.

Can't shut Janice and Candy out. Anna mutters at them, Janice squawks, brushes something off her leg, something live that drops to the ground and scuttles off, and Janice fires a bilious glare at Anna, as if she's to blame.

Anna ignores it. She tries to listen to Véronique, and it's Silowa who makes room for her against the bank of the gully, so she can get closer and hear better . . .

Now picture this, Véronique is saying. *The bank of a seasonal stream. During the rains, it drains from high ground into the lake. Acacia trees give it shade in the heat of the day (like your camp at Chomlaya). The lake is full of fish; its green margins throng with animals. Human-like creatures – they are like us, but they are not yet us – they gather here to camp. They fish. Cut up meat with stone tools. Eat. Strip bones, clean skins.*

Anna looks around. As if she's seeing it all. Silowa whispers; she nods, whispers back . . .

From time to time (Véronique is raising her voice above the grumbling from Candy), *heavy rain in the hills flows down, swelling the stream. It breaks above its banks, just a little. Maybe the rains come early, catching our creatures by surprise. They abandon camp for high ground. They leave tools behind: flaked cobbles, whittled sticks, animal hides, bones, fishheads, eggshells, tubers, bits and pieces of rubbish. They move on, out of our story. Anybody noticed how sand on a seashore shifts with the tides?*

Murmurs all round. Véronique is pleased. She continues, *So, the abandoned camp is flooded. Think of water lapping over, just softly covering everything with silt. In time, more and more silt settles on top; everything but the bone and the stone decay. As hundreds of thousands of years go by, the silt hardens to rock . . .* She's leading them along the gully towards the outcrop of rocks, Anna and Silowa in front. *I have said to you, 'Imagine this'. But . . .* Véronique stops, *it is true. It is a story told in the sides of this gully. There is no lake now. Almost nothing grows here because there is little rainfall. But there are flash floods, and these are our gift. They erode the soil. Year after year they cut down through millions of years of sediments and – gradually, gradually – evidence for our story emerges . . .*

Between the rocks she marches them, and suddenly there it is: long trenches in the earth, people kneeling, peering, brushing, digging, hoisting buckets, sieving, picking, spreading, sorting . . .

Each and every one of us here, maybe even one of you today – will put a little bit of that story together. We're on a quest! For what? Guess!

Everyone looks at everyone else, except for Anna, who's watching a man kneeling down and brushing something in the soil, delicately, with a small paint-brush. He glances from under an enormous hat at her. He beckons her to look closer.

An exaggerated sigh from Candy ascends in the silence. Zak, egged on by Antony, is the bold one.

Looking for hominids?

Our ancestors . . .? Antony joining in.

Ancestors, hominids! Got it! So, here's the story: our evolution – human evolution – started with an ape. Over millions of years, some evolved that were less ape-like, more human-like; some stood up on their hind legs. We're the only hominid living on Earth today. How did we become what we are? It's a treasure hunt! And it starts with something like this . . .

She signals to Silowa. He's like a magician conjuring a rabbit: a flourish and he holds up a fragment – small, flat, dark, then it catches sunlight, becomes glossy, burnished brown, like polished wood.

Piece of skull, announces Véronique. *Silowa here has the wonderful sharp eyes that spotted this one! A tiny, tiny piece of fossilized skull. Much, much older than our creatures by the stream. Three and a half million years old (give or take a few hundred thousand years). Here's another piece, and another. Silowa is helping Dr Otaka here* (the kneeling man in the hat raises a hand) *to put the pieces together. Just like a jigsaw. And so we will start to know what this individual looked like.*

Silowa's showing the fossil to Anna. The two of them, heads together, chattering like they've been friends for years.

Later, under awnings billowing in the hot wind, tables spread with thousands of bone fragments. Proudly Silowa lists them: *Giraffe. Hippo. That is big – antelope – like the eland. That*

*is a pig. That is human. Thigh bone. Footbones. Toes. Everything
gives clues! Stone tool! Bone! I am learning about it. These ones are
older than a million years – the layer of the rock tells us this! You go
across the ground like this,* he's demonstrating, loping like an
antelope, long-legged and skinny, but he's quartering the
ground, scanning as he goes, *like looking for pieces of gold . . .
you see these little changes in colour. Come, I show you.*

Off to a rubble-covered slope nearby – Anna, but also
Matt, Joe, Zak, Antony, Tamara. Pebbles across the surface, red
and grey and black, and Silowa swoops, lifts something: a
nobble of bone. *See, you just look and look again, and then again.
This is common, this bone. They lie on the surface, hundreds, all
over. They were buried, but now the rain and the wind have taken
the top of the soil away and they are just there, you can pick them
up. Me,* he declares, *me, I will find something not common. I will
find something to wonder at!*

'So,' the inspector probed, 'then Silowa comes to Chomlaya to
see you?'

'On the supply lorry from Burukanda.'

'And you share Silowa's fascination for these bones?'

'Working out what they are, *when* they're from – that's
pretty good,' Joe said slowly. 'Anna and Silowa, they're mad

about searching for them . . .'

He stopped. Something had risen and fallen again in his mind, and then there was only the inspector and Ella again, waiting expectantly for something more, and the sergeant and Tomis, already walking back towards them.

An imperceptible shake of the head passed between the sergeant and the inspector.

'The path is good,' Tomis announced to them all. 'It goes up high, high! I am impressed that Silowa has found it. I will ask him how he sniffs this out!'

But Joe, scrabbling to hold a thread in his thoughts, felt it slipping away. 'There's Anna's logbook,' he told them, 'she draws things we saw . . .'

Startled, the inspector glanced at the sergeant. 'I have not seen any logbook of Anna's.'

'We have found only the books which you have, Sir. No personal –'

'We all had to write them,' Joe insisted. 'Miss Strutton made it a competition.'

'No writing books of this sort in the missing students' tents. I am certain of this, Sir,' asserted the sergeant. 'But I will investigate. They are perhaps with the teacher, and she has not seen fit to show them to us.'

'We could ask everyone,' Ella pointed out. Again she had been watching the camp below. The canteen tent was clearly visible, a drift of figures assembling in the open space around it.

'Well,' declared the inspector, getting up. 'I detect Miss Strutton's meeting is about to take place. Yes, Ella, we can ask. In fact, we too can have a meeting! Joe, what you have told us has been very good, very helpful. We should be encouraged! Now we return as fast as we can. And, Sergeant Kaonga, we will not just talk to *a few* people and upset our Miss Strutton a little bit. We will talk to everyone and upset her much more, because we will bar the teachers, particularly we will bar our argumentative Miss Strutton. She will not be able to hear what the students choose to say to us. And I will be very childish and enjoy this punishment!'

10 a.m.

Barely an hour we have taken to get back to the camp, Murothi thought, and already Miss Strutton has found tasks for everyone at the farthest corners of the camp. Does she deliberately thwart our chance to talk to people?

Now Tomis and the sergeant were rounding the students up.

Murothi unzipped his tent and went in. On the rickety table, in a pile at the back, the students' *Book Of Days* and the official teachers' log; on the right, typed transcripts of taped police interviews with all six teachers and the two rangers: Tomis Ntonye and Likon Soimara. Next to them, handwritten notes of police conversations with the camp cook, Samuel Lekitumu, and the two expedition drivers: David Ntanyaki and Nicolas Waiputari. All three were away from the camp on the day of the disappearances. Samuel and Nicolas were buying vegetables, chickens and goat meat from the villages. Their routes had been confirmed by many people, and that they returned after the police search had begun.

No mysteries there.

No mystery either about David Ntanyaki, who had driven the large group of students and teachers on the overnight expedition to Lengoi Hot Springs. This was the group that included Ian Boyd. He scanned Ian Boyd's interview again. He is one I must speak to, after the students, he thought. At breakfast, he seems to have a desire to talk, yet now he is nowhere to be seen. And what of the other teachers? In his return through the camp, Murothi had noted that not one of these was in sight. In fact, not one of these had shown any inclination to speak to Murothi either on his arrival at the camp yesterday afternoon, or in the few hours of this morning.

They manage to lose three children. Yet they behave as if it is not their responsibility to find them. Their interviews say *nothing*.

He put aside the notes on the six teachers, and Samuel, Nicolas and David.

That left Tomis and Likon.

Tomis Ntonye (TN)
Date: 24/2/06
Time: 18.35
Place: Northern Province. Chomlaya, British Student Camp
Interviewed by Sergeant Adewa Kaonga (AK),
Constable Lasitai Lakuya (LL): Nanzakoto Police

Department.

Case No: 06574

Tape reference: 2006/Chomlaya/16

AK   Explain your role here, please.

TN   I am a game ranger, and the guide here - there are two of us. Likon Soimara is also here. We take the visitors to places, and we tell them about everything.

AK   You know these missing students?

TN   I know all the students here, of course, of course! I have been working at this camp since everyone arrived. Three weeks now. I know these missing ones very well. They are noticeable! Matt is very interested in what I tell him about animals. He is inventing some music. He wants to listen to the animal cries and make music notes so they echo each other. He is full of questions. They are all full of questions - questions, questions. It is interesting for me.

AK   And Silowa?

TN   Silowa is their good friend. He comes to see them at the camp, he is with them whenever he can stay. At first he goes away at night. But then he stays. He persuades Samuel Lekitumu -

AK   Samuel Lekitumu? He is here? I have not seen

him yet. I know him well!

TN   He is a good man. A good man. He lets Silowa sleep in the store tent. The store tent is Samuel's kingdom, so the teachers cannot say yes or no!

AK   I see. Tell me more about Silowa.

TN   This is a boy with many ideas. Big plans. He sees many adventures ahead! I wish I had ideas like this boy when I was young. You know he has three years in school, but he is going to get himself back to school and gain all the higher examinations. He says this to me. I believe him. He will do it! His people are pastoral. They do not have the school fees any more. He tells me that he comes to the Burukanda archaeology camp with his uncle. The herders bring news of any erosion sites that they see. It may help the scientists. They get payment for doing it. They get a good meal. They enjoy the visit. A very good get-together! The herders are good scouts. Eyes like the eagle! Silowa talks about all this many times. He talks many times to everybody - to me, to Likon Soimara, to Nicolas Waiputari, to lots of the students - to these missing ones in particular but to others, too. But after they travel to

Kasinga, he talks to other people less, and stays with the missing ones only. I think they start to keep away from the others.

AK   The trip to Kasinga? What is important about this?

TN   Joe and Matt and Anna go on this journey and Silowa persuades Likon to let him go too. Likon is happy to agree. There is room in the vehicles. He likes Silowa. He is also happy for Silowa's other friend to join the expedition.

AK   Who is this other friend?

TN   Ndigi. He is another boy who works now and then at Burukanda. He becomes a good friend with Matt. They are mad, very mad, they are just like each other: mad about inventing music! Ndigi has made Matt a pipe.

AK   And why does everyone go to Kasinga? What is there?

TN   The students will help build a schoolroom and dig some wells. The readers of Charly's newspaper, they help to pay for the cement and these kinds of things. It is part of this expedition. This was just the first visit to Kasinga, to meet the people there.

AK   Silowa goes too, but after this he does not talk to other students. Why is this?

TN   Charly says to me that there was something nasty happening. She was angry, she said it was shaming. This was the word she used. She was ashamed of the teachers - that they do nothing. She did not explain. You can maybe ask Likon. He went with them but he was in the other vehicle. Me, I just notice that Silowa, Matt, Joe, Anna, sometimes Ndigi when he is here, keep far from other people after this day.

AK   Tomis, when was this?

TN   A week ago, Friday. . . yes. You can see in the logbook. This teacher, Miss Strutton, writes down what is done every day.

AK   OK. So, when was the last time you saw the students who have vanished?

TN   They are here when we leave to drive to Lengoi. They are gone when we come back. Charly is also gone. It all happens when we are far.

Murothi stopped reading, and quickly picked up the students' log, *The Book Of Days*. He skimmed for the entry he half-remembered.

There it was:

23 February. Tamara (Buffalos).

We all had to get up in the dark for breakfast at first light and the Buffalos were supposed to be ready to leave for the trip to Lengoi Hot Springs but then Guess Who? got thrown off at the last minute! Miss Strutton picked out Katra and Andy and Phil from the Antelopes to go instead, and they hadn't got packed, so we hung about, played cards, got bored, got more bored, played more cards.

Quickly, the names in each team? He rifled through the police notes, found the list, ran his eyes down. Buffalos: fifteen names including the girls who spoke to Joe at breakfast, Tamara and Janey, and the boys they mentioned, Zak and Antony. Joe, Matt and Anna, also on the list.

But Joe, Matt and Anna did not go to Lengoi. They were left in the camp with – he found the list of Antelopes: fifteen names, among them, Sean and his friends. The sergeant had checked the names for him: Denny and Carl.

Joe and Matt and Anna in the camp without Tamara, Janey, Zak, Antony too, who appeared to be friends. Without Ian Boyd. Without Charly.

Is this *significant*?

Trying not to rush, Murothi checked meticulously through the other interviews. Lawrence Sharp, one of the teachers who had been in the camp all the time: same questions about when the disappearances were noticed, and how. Answers: alert at about midday, when the three students were sent for and did not come. No search until the Lengoi group returned, because *Miss Strutton thought it was unnecessary, she said the students were just avoiding their duties.* The only other teacher there, Miss Hopper, sounded like a parrot; it could have been Miss Strutton speaking. Perhaps a little less strident.

He picked up the Elisa Strutton interview, leafing through it, hearing her voice and tone rising off the paper, as if she stood in front of him now with her pert smile switched on and off like clockwork.

ES   They were given the task of digging a new trench.

DC   Where was this?

ES   At the back of the camp. For the toilets. The old trench was damaged during the storm three nights ago, the sides broke down. We need to fill it in and dig a new one.

DC   Who else was doing this?

ES   Just those three.

Just those three. Kitchen duties, digging trenches. Punishment duties. All inside the camp, not outside. Inside, inside. The trouble comes from *inside* –

'Inspector,' Tomis's head poked through the tent door, 'the students are there. Sergeant Kaonga is with them, and the constables are keeping the teachers at a long arm's length! Everything is ready for you.'

'And our other two youngsters?'

'I have sent Joe to his tent to recover from the climb. He is not well, this is clear. Ella too. We must be careful, she is not accustomed to the heat. Likon and I will keep watch over them. Inspector Murothi, there will be no wandering off to get lost!'

In the dark green interior of the tent there was an illusion of coolness. Joe dropped on to the camp-bed. The climb had flattened him.

But he dared not sleep. Even the canvas overhead resonated with the pulse of his dreams. He was afraid to close his eyes.

Yet, during the climb up Chomlaya with the policemen and Tomis and Ella, he had begun to feel lighter: expectant, even. As if the little memories were conjuring Anna and Matt and Silowa from the solid walls of Chomlaya; as if any moment they would walk down the path, chattering, and all the horror of their absence would be revealed as some peculiar, shared hallucination.

Now, though, the camp sucked hope away. Something

desolate and bleak reasserted itself. He felt watched, yet alone; snared by the twilight of the tent, bereft, weighted by something he should know about his friends, but did not.

He knew the raw, inescapable possibility of their deaths.

There was a shift in the air beside him, a change in the refraction of light. Again, something swung on the edge of his vision, swung and turned and turned again, and a sweat broke from him, cold – a terror from somewhere else, deep in the murk of obscured memory. The thing was real, it had swung there, *here*, when they were all *here*, not in Charly's tent, *here* . . .

He steeled himself, turned his head, slowly.

Nothing. Flare of light through the opening; dark, framing angles of canvas. Logic told him it could not be here, this was a new tent, raised only last night when he arrived with Ella and the inspector.

Then the brightness through the entrance dimmed, he braced against it, yelled at what might step through.

It was only Ella, bending, peering in at him. He wiped his face with his hands. He felt stupid, saw she looked embarrassed, even shy. He pulled a face: half-smiled at her, shamefaced at his cry, like a kid getting scared.

She said quickly, 'Are you OK? You shouted . . .'

But he didn't answer because her voice came to him lifted on the song of a pipe, Matt's pipe –

'Hear that?' he asked urgently.

'What?'

'The pipe. There – music . . .'

She listened, carefully.

'There's a bird . . . can't hear music . . . it sounds a bit like a pipe . . .' Doubtfully.

But its call tugged him, the physical wrench of a cord. At the same time the doubt in her voice showed that it was his own private delusion, no different from the tilting of the ground he had felt before or the echo pulsating in his bones. And as he thought this, the trembling sound ceased. There was only Ella's persistent, 'Joe, *Joe*, are you feeling sick? What's wrong?' and she'd pushed right into the tent, knelt down to look into his face.

'Sorry,' he said. 'Just feeling weird. Didn't sleep last night . . .'

'Maybe it's heatstroke, too. Here, drink. Like Tomis said, you have to drink. Lots.' She pushed his water bottle at him. 'Come on, Joe! You should sleep, too. There's nothing else happening while the inspector talks to everyone.'

Obediently, he drank. Then he said, grimacing at the

ridiculousness of it, 'Dreams – you know, nightmare things . . .'
He laughed, self-conscious, and she saw, as clear as anything,
that he was afraid.

'If you like,' she offered, 'I'll hang about for a bit . . . I'm not
doing anything. I'll just sit outside . . . you know, and you can
sleep – I'll wake you up if anything happens.'

He didn't answer. Just looked at her for a minute, and then
lay down, and appeared to Ella to be instantly asleep.

She didn't move straightaway. She stood looking at him.
He was sprawled on the camp-bed, just as he'd let himself fall
back. Every few minutes his face flickered and he turned his
head in agitation. She had the impulse to soothe him, as she'd
wanted to in the hospital, that first night. But that seemed a
lifetime away, and she hadn't even known him then.

This, suddenly, was different. She knew him now. All the
feelings she'd had – the shared fear, the desolation, the lost look
that came over his face – washed over her. She wanted to put
her arms round him. She wanted his arms round her. It was a
feeling she'd never had before, and for a moment it obscured
everything else in her mind.

Then she was stricken by how long she'd stood there: he'd
wake, read her face, be embarrassed by what it said, want her to
go away.

She ducked out of the tent, into blinding sunlight.

There was a crackle, which she recognised as the static of a radio, and she looked towards the police vehicles. One of the constables was leaning in and lifting a handset, speaking into it, his voice carrying, but the language meaningless to her.

The constable put the handset down, and leaned in the shade of the great squat baobab. Beyond him, the makeshift encampment sheltering the local helpers was just visible among the acacia trees. A single figure moved across the front. Otherwise it was still. Was it because people had moved to help search on the north side of the ridge, or were they dispersing, going home, giving up?

The thought iced the sweat on her back, and a wash of sour fear churned her stomach. She turned back and looked into the tent. Joe had rolled on to his side, facing away towards the canvas wall. He was lying still and seemed calmer.

She busied herself, repositioning pegs and guy ropes to make the flap of the tent into an awning against the relentless force of the sun. And then she sat cross-legged in the patch of shade, to wait.

She felt Sean before she saw him. Not quite a shadow, not quite a sound, not quite a movement. He was motionless, at the corner of the tent. Clearly he had not expected to see her there. But surprise was swiftly stripped from his face as she looked up. He smiled. A broad smile that Ella would have found quite friendly, had she not already experienced Joe's reaction to him at breakfast, or the ambush by his two friends.

He crouched down very close to her, putting his hand on her shoulder, companionably.

'Ella, right?' he said. 'Charly's sister, yeah? Friend of Joe's?'

It was not a pleasant feeling, his height. Even squatting, he loomed over her, and she had a sudden very clear knowledge that he enjoyed this. He was so close she could feel the heat of his skin. He was sweating, and there was a faintly perfumed, faintly oiled smell on his arms.

Why was he here, in Joe's tent when everyone was called to the inspector's meeting?

She jumped to her feet, deliberately dislodging Sean's hand. 'Joe's sleeping!'

'Yeah? Tired, is he? With all the stuff he's trying to remember? Do your head in, that would, not remembering. What's he said?'

As he spoke he moved, blocking her route to Joe, one hand resting on the ridge pole of the tent, the other hooked in his waistband. He bent his knees suddenly, making a show of crouching to look directly into her face, raising an eyebrow.

She stared past him to avoid his gaze. With a lurch, she saw he was not alone. Two boys: his friends. Keeping watch. She threw caution to the winds and went for counter-attack, glaring at him. 'What're you doing here?'

His smile didn't alter. His hand though, moved from his waistband back to her shoulder, the grip harder, fingers heavy. He said, 'Well, could ask you the same, couldn't I? What're you doing? Poor Joe's armed guard?'

She flushed. 'Inspector Murothi's talking to everyone in the camp –'

'He's not talking to me, is he?'

'Well, you're supposed –'

'I'm not *supposed* to do anything.'

'Sean!' One of the boys beckoned urgently.

Sean ignored him. He kept his eyes on Ella. 'Tell your mate Joe here, with the empty brain that doesn't *remember* anything, he should –'

'I'm not telling Joe anything,' she said stoutly. 'He's recovering. And Inspector Murothi's looking after him. *All the time.*'

'Not *all* the time, eh? Sometimes it's his brave little helper.'

She threw off his hand, took a step back, and dodged

sideways so that she blocked the entrance to the inner tent.

He laughed, considered her for a moment, stepped closer, calling over his shoulder, 'Hey, Denny, got that knife?'

'Course not! I'm not stupid. There's police all over!'

'Fetch it.'

'Look, I'm off, there's Tomis. *Sean!*' Rapidly the other two were walking away, already out of sight as Tomis appeared and Sean ambled away, deliberately slowly, in full view of the ranger.

Tomis tossed his head in their direction. He raised his hand to Ella, called loudly, 'I am the herdsman rounding up stray goats! Is all well with you?'

'Yes,' she said. 'A few goats went that way.'

He chuckled, acknowledging her joke. 'I see one. Two others also?'

She nodded. He set off after them, giving her the thumbs up.

Ella stayed where she was. How could she have let Sean's pathetic effort at a threat frighten her? How could he do anything, anyway, with the inspector, and the sergeant, and Tomis and Samuel here?

It wasn't what he did, or said – not even the talk of a knife, you couldn't take that seriously! But she saw what he believed, his vision of himself: outside it all, beyond reach. He didn't *care*.

She was on edge, reluctant to sit down, alert for his return.

Silence descended on the camp. Only the lethargic drone of insects, the breath-sucking heat buzzing on the plain. She caught a twitch of movement and turned her head. A gecko, like a white lizard-ghost pinned in alarm against the canvas . . . *geckos and frogs and lizards camouflaged so completely you almost never spot them*, Charly had mentioned. And she'd written about the archaeology and Burukanda, everything Joe had been telling them . . .

Ella pulled Charly's emails from her pocket, and sat down again.

From: charlyT@hotmail.com
To: ellaT@hotmail.com
Sent: Saturday, 18 February, 2006, 17:37
Subject: More notes from Chomlaya

Now I'VE got the bug! Actually, Elly, I'm not joking. I got a real prickle up my spine when I was handed a skull and I stood looking down at it, into that bony, hollow face, and thought, 'you might be my ancestor from 4 million years back'. It started me sort of understanding the mood I feel in Chomlaya. There's something so ageless and forever about it. You can imagine people like the skull person, as if their spirits, over millions and millions of years, are all still in the air. Weird, wild nonsense, eh?

Got to keep to facts, Charly - like a good journalist.

Well, thought you'd find this pretty interesting (there's a girl here who reminds me a bit of you, Elly, and she's fascinated!). So, the facts (courtesy of what I've learned from my Burukanda friends, Véronique and Otaka - you'll meet them when you come, I'm determined):

1) What they do know: human evolution started with an ape, taking millions of years, some apes evolving that were less ape-like and more human-like, and some standing up on their hind legs (all these - humans and upright-walking near-humans, are called hominids, by the way). Could be an extinct ancestor of ours, or a relative that developed on a separate branch, or a true human, becoming a modern human (the only hominid living on Earth now). All humans are hominids. Not all hominids are humans.

From the fossils, they know the first hominids were still small-brained and ape-like, and they evolved in Africa somewhere between 7 and 8 million years ago - we last shared a common ancestor with the chimpanzee round about then. By about 2 million years ago, there's a species we can actually recognise as human with a bigger brain.

2) But here's what they don't know: what exactly happened between those dates: 7 and 2 million years ago? Haven't found enough fossils to tell how each type developed, how many hominid species lived and died, and WHICH OF THEM evolved a much larger brain. That's what everyone at Burukanda's doing – filling in a bit of the missing shape of the human family tree. What hominid species lived? How? HOW did WE (WHY did WE, of all other animals on earth) evolve from ONE of those strands to develop language, artistic imagination, technological innovation?

Intriguing, eh? I might volunteer for a month or three of hard work on the dig some time, find out what it's like. Fancy coming with me, Elly, one summer? Let's do it! As I said, there are a few students here who're equally fascinated by it – though they have to contend with Our Leader who thinks fossils are unhygienic so she dumped them in the lavatory trench! The dreaded lady hasn't invaded my space yet, but I wouldn't put it past her. Beginning to wonder if I need to watch what I write and where I leave my notes!

Got to finish, Elly! Vehicle's about to head

off for Ulima, and I want them to send this for
me, soonest. Next instalment in a few days.
      xxxxxxCxxxxxx

Ella halted. Trying not to rush it, she went back a few sentences.
*Beginning to wonder if I need to watch what I write and where I
leave my notes!*

Charly's notes! Where are they? She'd have pages and
pages of notes! The inspector never said anything about notes!

What's happened to Charly's *notebook*?

Heart hammering, Ella leapt up, rushed into the tent, and
woke Joe.

11 a.m.

Murothi surveyed the students across the canteen tent. They sat on tables and benches or squatted on the grass between. At his arrival, a wary silence spread from group to group.

They measure me, he thought. *I am an unpredictable animal. They watch to see which way I will jump.* And something more – the air was polluted with undercurrents – he smelled it as surely as a poisonous stench.

Sergeant Kaonga was breathing heavily, pulling a handkerchief from his pocket, mopping beads of sweat from his face. 'Tomis is hunting the boy Sean and his friends. They believe they do not need to attend your meeting. And Likon is doing a lion's work, facing Miss Strutton.'

Murothi took the list of names from him: fifteen boys, fifteen girls. The sergeant had ticked the ones who were already here – twenty-two in all – and crossed the five missing ones: Sean, Janice, Candy, Carl, Denny. Three were unmarked: Joe, Anna and Matt.

He allowed his eyes to drift casually over the heads of the students; a muted buzz of conversation had resumed. He remarked, 'Sergeant Kaonga, I have some new thoughts. I will tell you about them afterwards. I would like to know what you think.'

'And I have spoken to the climbers,' the other man reported. 'Where they are now, the radio communication is very bad across the rock. They are near where Joe was discovered. Nothing more has been seen, I am very sorry to say – Hoi!' he broke off, glancing past Murothi. 'They are here.'

It was Tomis, and beside him, with an air of offhand boredom, Sean. The four others trailed behind, all talking loudly. As if the world must be interested in what they say, thought Murothi. He resisted the temptation to scrutinise them obviously. But an unexpected certainty settled in his mind. Somewhere in this conundrum of disappearances these five played a part.

They pushed through the throng, to the table furthest from the policemen. Murothi detected the reluctant ceding of space to them, some people even giving up their places completely and moving away. Clearly Sean and his friends were not to be refused. Even as Murothi mused on this, Sean caught his eye. The boy's gaze was purposeful; he did not shift his eyes on.

The effort at a challenge smacked of the games played by some grown men Murothi knew who liked to think they were all-powerful. Something deep in him tightened, became a little angry. Why is no adult stopping this? It is not difficult to see these undercurrents – the child, Ella, has seen them already!

Murothi raised a hand of acknowledgment to Tomis, and stood up. An instantaneous, keyed-up silence greeted him.

'Well, you will know,' he began, 'that there is very, very great urgency to find your friends. By the time the sun sets tonight, it will be nearly five days since they vanished –'

Unexpectedly this produced a muted shuffling, like a preparation for something, and he paused, surprised. But almost at once the unrest subsided, and all eyes fixed on him again. Even Sean's.

'The search has been extensive: even now the helicopters are ranging over a wide area and ground searches are being made on and round the rocks. Climbers are on the north face of Chomlaya, where Joe was found two days ago. Unfortunately, as you know, Joe cannot remember how he got there.'

There were sudden loud voices behind the policemen, among them, Miss Strutton's. Several students stood up, craning their necks to look.

'Concentrate!' Murothi's raised voice snapped their attention back. 'I know you have already been interviewed. But I have asked you here again, because you may have knowledge that you do not *know* you have. The smallest thing! Think! Even guess! What could these people be going to do when they left this camp?'

The blank stares were like a wall.

'Or perhaps you know who they were going to see?'

The silence altered: shock.

'You mean someone maybe *took* them?' This from near the front, close to Murothi. Everyone else looked towards the speaker, and then back at Murothi.

'I do not mean anything,' he said. The evident surprise told him the students had not imagined this. 'At this point we do not know anything, except where they have *not* been found. We do not even know *when* they left the camp – by choice or in any other way. Do *any* of you have an answer to this?'

Across the group there was a ruffle of shaking heads, but still no words, and Murothi suppressed a sigh. Were English children always this reluctant to speak?

If you are on the road to nowhere, Murothi, find another road.

All eyes continued to watch him intently.

'Who are friends to the missing students? Close friends?'

There was a tightening of the atmosphere. Why should such an obvious question provoke unease?

Two hands went up: he recognised the girls who had

spoken to Joe at breakfast: Janey and Tamara. Then another hand, and then several more. Five altogether, and then, just as he finished taking this in, a sixth.

'Now we are getting somewhere,' Murothi said briskly. 'Thank you. Sergeant Kaonga and I would like to talk to you afterwards. Now, I am told these missing ones were often in trouble.'

'Yeah, and they've run off, haven't they?' A single voice, loud, from the direction of Sean, but Murothi did not think it was his.

Fiercely, Janey countered, 'They just got blamed for stuff that wasn't them.'

Suddenly there was a low murmur, seeming to ripple out in concentric rings around Sean's group. A few people glanced over their shoulders.

'It's true,' asserted Janey defiantly, '*isn't it, Tamara?*'

'Too right,' yelled someone else, Tamara's emphatic nod matched unexpectedly by an explosion of several voices . . .

'– *someone hung this disgusting thing, dead, so the hyenas came –*'

'– *leopard, not just hyenas –*'

'– *Miss said it was Matt –*'

'– *they got pulled off going to Lengoi –*'

There was an intake of breath, fanned by a drift of whispering and something that Murothi could not quite pin down, like a shifting of rows within the haphazard scattering of students. Sean and his friends, initially in a solid knot of people, were a little more visible: Sean looking around with studied indifference, Candy and Janice head to head, talking, Denny and Carl bending forward, speaking to the people in front.

'They whisper in people's ears; they try to rule, Sir,' commented Sergeant Kaonga quietly.

'I see it.' Again Murothi addressed the students. 'Explain. What was hung? Where? When? Quickly, now.'

'In the night. Before we went to Lengoi.' The answer came from Tamara.

'Little antelope thing – a dik dik,' volunteered a boy sitting beside her. He was one who had identified himself as a friend. 'Stuck up in this tree behind Matt and Joe's tent. Samuel and Tomis took it out into the bush so the vultures would eat it. They said in the camp it would bring animals in, and that's dangerous. They were angry!'

'Angry with . . . ?'

The boy shrugged. 'Whoever did it.'

'And who was that?'

Another blanketing stillness.

Finally, 'Dunno.' From somewhere to the boy's left came a scornful snort. He continued doggedly, 'Miss Strutton said it was them – Matt and Joe and Anna – to make the animals get close to their tent so Matt could hear the sounds for his music.'

'Ah! And you know it was not them?'

Energetic nods from several quarters.

'And there were other times like this?'

No answer.

'Pay very close attention to me,' vigorously Murothi threw his voice across the gathering, 'These missing people may *die* because we do not get information *in time to locate them*. Every minute, every hour counts. This is no time for secrets or games.'

Promisingly, a girl who had not claimed to be a friend, volunteered, 'They started going off all the time with Silowa, so we don't know . . .'

'They did not go on the expeditions with you?'

'At first, yeah, but after that fight . . .' The girl flushed suddenly, looked across at Candy, and stopped.

'Fight?' Murothi prompted.

'I wasn't there,' she said hastily, 'just heard. It was on the Land Cruiser – when they went to Kasinga. Ask Joe.'

'Does anyone else know about this?'

'– *something about seats and that. About Silowa* –'

'– *called him names –*'

'– *stupid stuff. Anna went crazy –*'

Murothi spoke carefully, recalling those sentences in Tomis's interview: *Charly said there was something nasty happening . . . she said it was shaming.*

'So, it was stupid, but it upset Anna?'

'Well, *some people* tried to stop Silowa going. Miss Strutton started it. Because she went and pulled down Matt's tent and that, didn't she, when . . .' the girl looked round her for support, and Murothi understood he was very close to something.

The girl did not go on.

'I am confused,' said Murothi. 'Dead animals in trees. Fights. Is this Anna's way, to fight?'

'No! Never!'

'So, things are said,' he spoke slowly. 'Are things also *done?*'

You could have heard the scuttle of a spider.

'Truly, silence is speech, Sir,' murmured Sergeant Kaonga. 'And what of this teacher's strange pulling down of tents?' Pursued by Likon and both constables, Miss Strutton was heading angrily towards them.

'. . . *utterly unacceptable, I'll have you know! I will not allow it!*'

'Sergeant,' Murothi said urgently, 'do whatever you can to

get her away. She is just a bully, and she cannot bully us.'

Sean, however, rose, stretched, elbowed his way through the students, began to saunter towards her.

'Sean,' Murothi kept his voice quiet, 'I believe that is your name – return to your seat. My discussion with all of you is not over.'

'Yeah, but –'

'Return, or I will conclude that you are obstructing my investigation and I will wonder why.'

A look of sudden, sullen fury flooded the boy's face. Simultaneously, Miss Strutton's voice, till now continuing in argument with both the sergeant and the constables, shut off. She could be seen marching away.

A flutter of something – nerves, thought Murothi, surprise that she is defeated – passed through the students. Sean hesitated. Then he pushed back to his seat.

He has the intelligence to see which way the wind blows, Murothi thought. It is no more than that.

'You *are* going to find them, Sir? I mean, in the end you are going to find them, right?' Tamara said.

The young faces surrounding her were now unmistakably scared.

'We do not know how Joe reached the other side of

Chomlaya. But he was there, and this gives great hope that the others may be there, too, or near it. This is why I ask you to tell us anything, anything at all that may help to direct the helicopters and climbers. Now, two final things. You write accounts of your days here – personal accounts. I wish to look at them.'

'Miss Strutton's got them. She's looking at them for the competition.'

'Aha – this competition again. It occupies a very great deal of your time here, I see! Well, thank you. You may all go. Except those close friends we will speak to, and,' he paused, deliberately, 'Sean.'

The general hubbub could not obscure the alert coursing through the ranks, particularly the ranks of Sean's four friends.

Sean strolled forward.

Murothi had called the boy on impulse, and was not immediately clear what he should do.

He asked, 'Before the disappearances, when did you last see Joe?'

'Dunno. Didn't notice.'

'Matt? Anna?'

'Same.'

'At supper on the evening before they disappeared?'

'Don't remember.'

'What did you do that evening. After the meal?'

A whisper of a pause. 'Played cards. Hung about.'

'Hung about? What does this mean?'

'Didn't do much.'

'And where did you do this hanging about?'

'Here. Like everyone. In the canteen.'

'Till what time?'

'Usual time.'

'Be precise.'

'Nine.'

'And then?

'We go to our tents. Rules. The big lamps go off.'

Murothi contemplated him. The boy contemplated him back, a direct, unblinking stare.

Very unafraid, thought Murothi. Very *annoyed*.

'You may go,' he said suddenly. A flush came to Sean's face; he did not at once comply. Then he pushed unnecessarily between Janey and Tamara and several others waiting for Murothi. Equally deliberately, they did their best not to notice.

Murothi checked the notes of the conversation he'd just had with Tamara, Janey, Zak, Antony, Gideon, Henry.

Confirmed – the missing ones were at supper. They sat apart. Afterwards they didn't stay with everyone else round the fire. Silowa was not there. Not one single person saw any of them at breakfast.

These missing ones are bullied, he thought. By students and by a teacher. This trouble is inside, not outside the camp.

But still I have *nothing* to explain why they leave, telling no one. Why the journalist also leaves, later, in the middle of a searing day. Why Joe alone returns. Nothing to say *where they are.*

It was nearly midday. He tried to block out the refrain pounding through his head. *We will not discover these missing people. Or we will discover them too late.*

He felt the old dismay threatening. *Do not let this poisoned air stifle you, Murothi. We must blow it away.*

The place was just as Charly described it. Even in the scorch of midday, there was the whisper of reeds, trickle of water, cool air above moist sand.

'Why do you think Charly'd hide something here?' Joe asked. 'Wouldn't she leave everything in the tent?'

'See, if Charly's notes were in her tent the police would've seen them, wouldn't they? The inspector would've *told* me.

Maybe she's said in her notes what you were doing, Joe, or – I don't know, *something*. I keep thinking WHY would she go off like that, not telling anyone, when she knew you were lost? It's not like her, it's just NOT – she MUST'VE known where you went and thought you were all right!'

Did she? Joe looked away, avoiding Ella's eyes. Charly wasn't there that last night. I do know that. *The night before the unknown thing happened, at the unknown time, and we went to the unknown place.* Charly went to Burukanda in the morning, early – before anyone was up –

A memory surfaced: Charly stooping into Anna's tent to call her out. Taking her beyond earshot of the other girls. Anna and Charly whispering, outlined in pale dawn light . . .

'. . . and then,' Ella's voice insisted, 'there's what Charly wrote about coming to this place –'

'Child, child, I am sure you are right, I am sure you are right,' broke in Samuel, calming. With Constable Lesakon he had led the way here to the tiny beach on the bend of the stream. 'Charly is many times sitting here, writing. If she does not wish to leave something in the camp, it is very possible she hides it in this place.' He regarded the constable thoughtfully. 'Ndoto my friend, it seems to me the child is right.'

'Samuel, explain this to me. Why –?'

'Look.' Ella showed them Charly's email: *Beginning to wonder if I need to watch what I write and where I leave my notes!* 'Charly's notes – they're – well – important, she never throws any of them away, she's got shelves and shelves of notebooks from everything she writes. There's private things in them too, like a diary. If she thought someone would take them –'

'This someone: who is this someone?' demanded the constable, frowning.

'Miss Strutton,' Ella said, and Samuel tilted his head in agreement.

'Ah!' said the constable. 'This Miss Strutton is one to steal the journalist's notes.'

'This Miss Strutton is one to demand to see through every door,' Samuel retorted. 'Even one that is not hers.' He heaved a sigh and lowered himself to a small flat-topped rock on the edge of the beach, stretching his legs wide and resting his hands on his knees. 'Yes, it is true. Charly likes to sit here.' He nodded. 'She likes to look at the light on Chomlaya's face.' He contemplated the razored heights of the ridge, the curl of the stream below, the mosaic of trees guarding its waters.

'Yes,' agreed Joe. He could hear them: Charly where Samuel sat now, and Silowa sprinting past, springing through water into sunlight, the boy's tall figure rustling through reeds to the rocks, scrape of Anna and Matt climbing behind, rasp of his own breath, scratch of pitted rock beneath fingers . . .

He felt Samuel watch him. The man turned, tracing the line of Joe's gaze across the stream. From here, the ravine carving down from Chomlaya's summit was masked by a tumble of giant boulders; you could not see the line of the splitting rock. But they both knew that one of Silowa's trails was there, winding deep into the echoing rift with its soaring russet walls and its perpetual clamour of birds.

'We climbed up there,' Joe said. 'Silowa knew all the ways up.'

'That way has been searched, I can tell you!' said the constable. 'I have been there. You go in, you come to these walls of big rock. Nowhere to go! The rock is breaking away all the time, in the big storm, some falls.'

'We knew not to go close to the cliffs,' said Joe. 'We only went a little way in, after the storm.' He remembered it boiling in the east, a vast green bruise on the horizon. Then a swirl of wind across the plains; a gasp, as if everything held its breath, the first fat drops of rain falling singly with thuds and plops, pitting the soil in miniature caverns. Then the storm breaking, ramming the camp like an avalanche, whipping trees to a frenzy, drenching everything, even under the canteen awning.

In the morning the air rinsed clean: a greening and gleaming of grass and leaves, a quickening trek of antelope and zebra and giraffe and buffalo through the dawn, and Silowa rushing to their tents, calling them to follow. Up on to the boulders, Anna and Matt and Joe kneeling beside him on the flattened top and looking over, following the line of his pointing finger. 'There, there.'

'What?' Matt shuffling closer to the edge.

'Oh, yeah, Silowa,' Anna breathes. 'Matt, look that way, to the side. Shh, Joe, don't lump about – you sound like an elephant!'

'Joe, they will feel you in the ground and slide away to hide,' Silowa's whispering and laughing. 'Anna is correct. You must be a feather on the ground!'

Edging to the rim, peeping over: a shallow pan of rock . . . bushes . . . a twitch of orange, black . . .

He shades his eyes. Sees the uncoiling loop, the angle of the head.

'A cobra?'

'Eee! We would not come near if it was a cobra! Me, I would be going very quietly away on the top of my toes! No, it is not a big, dangerous snake. See, it is many – father, mother, many many babies.'

What Joe has taken for a tail is a woven mesh of tiny snakes. Curling round them, a barricade against danger, is a larger one, and to one side, part-hidden below twiggy branches, another, not so big.

'See, it is the big mother who wraps herself round, and the little father who is beside. I have asked Likon the English name; it is sand boa,' announces Silowa, proud. 'They are bright with the rain and now they warm themselves in the sun.'

Joe watches the gleam of gold, fluid slide and ripple of purple-brown across the skin, the sinuous glide as the young snakes loop and weave and settle again.

But then there's that trickle of stones below, that grumble of human voices, and Matt's sudden alarm, 'It's Sean! And Carl!'

And Anna dodging back. 'Don't let them see us looking at the snakes! Don't let them see the snakes!'

'Why? It is interesting to see –'

'No, Silowa, no, you don't *know* them –'

Why remember this? Disgust crawled through Joe's stomach, and again something moved, at the edge of memory. When he turns his head to look, Silowa's hands lift it from the white soil . . .

He crouched down quickly, afraid he would fall. He tried to

explain to Samuel's curious face. 'It's nothing. Silowa just took us to see some snakes –'

Why remember it? His mouth went dry. He swallowed hard.

Worried, the constable interrupted, 'You are sick? You need to sit down? When the inspector comes from his meeting he will not be happy if we have let you be ill!'

'It's OK.' He went to the stream, splashed water across his face and into his mouth, wiping away the clammy aftermath of the nausea.

Samuel was still sitting. Slowly he was scrutinising their surroundings, as if his eyes would somehow light on what Charly might choose as a hiding place. Ella turned, eyes skimming, then began to walk from tree to tree, from bush to bush. The constable stomped to and fro, muttering to no one in particular and glancing at Joe every few steps as if afraid he might vanish between one glance and the next.

There were a million places – trees and branches, roots and boulders – offering hollows and hidden crevices.

'Be cautious,' Samuel called to Ella. She was reaching below a fallen tree trunk. 'Do not put your hand into things! This is a land of scorpions and spiders and snakes. They will not enjoy you invading their kingdom.'

'Oh!' said Ella, whipping her hand back, feeling stupid.

Joe went back and hunched down beside Samuel, copying him, looking at the place as Charly would see it: the scatter of boulders rimming the beach, the sparkle of water, the damp sand scoured by the traffic of animals and birds, and now by the constable's emphatic bootmarks.

He picked at the sand, lifting it, and letting it fall through his fingers. Here, where he squatted, the ground was ridged and broken – probably the marks of shoes scuffing moist soil, like Samuel's now. His eyes rested on it for a long, blank moment, and then he saw what was there.

He said, 'Here,' and pointed at the ground near the base of the small rock where Samuel sat.

Samuel contemplated it, and then he grunted. He heaved himself off and knelt down. He grasped the rock, and tipped it over.

In a hollow below, part-covered with sand, lay a square, flat, plastic-wrapped package.

Taking it from Samuel's outstretched hand, Ella's heart raced.

'You know your sister well, child,' commented Samuel, smiling. 'She will be proud. Ndoto! We have it!'

The constable looked up from his search, saw, and strode towards them.

Ella was unwrapping the bundle: a black bin bag; inside, a white carrier bag and inside that –

She stared at what she held. A fat, spiral-bound notebook, unmistakably Charly's – there was her familiar bold scrawl. But the other was not familiar: a hardbacked sketchbook, something written indecipherably on the front in orange bubble writing.

'That's Anna's!' exclaimed Joe, his tone puzzled.

Ella turned the pages. Sketches – some detailed and careful, others cartoon-like. Sharp, angular words scribbled here and there, as if Anna was angry. And on one page a series of caricatures: Miss Strutton, Sean, Denny, Carl, Janice, Candy. So unmistakable that Ella stared, amazed and impressed. All the teacher's pretty neatness was there. But she also had a look of gleeful madness, and she was dressed like those cartoons of cannibals who boil victims in cooking pots: a grass skirt with a bone through her high tight knot of hair. The page was headed *Savage Man and Savage Woman*, and the figures were all like that, in grass skirts or furry skins, expressions and features caught with a few swift, vicious strokes.

There they were again, on the next page: Denny was bludgeoning something with a club; Carl had skewered a bird on a stick; Candy and Janice were doing a jig; and Sean was dragging a girl to the party by the hair. Watching over it all was Strutton, but her head was turned and her face caught in horror at a tall figure approaching. It was Silowa, his shape and long braided hair recognisable from the photo Ella had, but Anna had also shaded his skin to show its blackness. He was smiling broadly and *welcome* burst from his mouth, but the words looping from Strutton's were, 'ARRGGGHH! *Help! A savage!*'

The next sheets had no cartoons, only detailed sketches of trees, careful labels filling the spaces in between: acacia thorn, olive, candle tree, fig tree, baobab . . .

'Please,' interrupted the constable, holding out his hand firmly. 'We will give these to the inspector. Now.'

Ella closed the book and handed it over, with Charly's. The constable tucked them under his arm, and gestured her and Joe towards the path.

Joe did not move. His gaze was travelling up on to the shoulder of Chomlaya and along, stopping at the point a few hundred metres away to their right, where the ridge began to curve away, out of sight.

'You must come,' the constable repeated. 'Now, now. You must not stay here to get lost! Back now. Into the camp, if you please! We must report to the inspector and the DC.'

Wordlessly, Joe shook his head.

'What is it?' the constable's voice rose with alarm.

Above, Ella could hear the shriek of a hawk. Joe looked towards it, and then at the drift of darker shapes in the distant sky. Ella knew they were vultures. She had a vision of them circling a carcass. Her heart began to thump uncontrollably.

Then Samuel spoke quietly to the constable, and touched her shoulder, and Joe's, and this time Joe responded, falling into step along the path. Behind, she heard Samuel murmur to Ndoto, 'The boy says nothing, but looks at this place all the time. He does not know why, I think. Perhaps he only *hears*, and it is not real. But the place should be looked at again. Ndoto, you must say this to the inspector and the sergeant. But let us do this very quickly and quietly. We do not encourage hope if there is only disappointment to come . . .'

Ahead, Joe was suddenly walking fast, almost running. He hadn't looked at her or spoken to her, and it seemed to Ella that he'd remembered something. It was bad. He wouldn't tell her because it was terrible, and now she stumbled frantically after him, unthinkable possibilities suddenly drowning all the hope that had flared only moments ago in finding Charly's book.

Joe had remembered nothing. He had heard the pipe. Not in dream, or memory, but here, now, spiralling upwards into the bleached-white sky. It seemed to call, as if Matt played it, this pipe that Silowa had given him, that Ndigi, Silowa's friend, had made.

Part of Joe knew it wasn't true.

Yet he could hear it, still. It sang and sang in the air around him. It rose higher and higher, sang and sang and sang, that somewhere, beyond the heights of Chomlaya, Matt was alive.

noon

Leaving the student meeting, Murothi was stopped by Likon, heavily out of breath from running. 'Inspector, I have to tell you – I did not think of it before, it was many days ago, but I remember just *now* when Tomis tells me of this talk with Joe about Silowa and bones –'

'Likon, it is all right,' Murothi quietened him. 'Recover your breath. Then you can tell me.'

The other breathed in, launched off again, 'It is this: Silowa, he wishes to talk to someone at Burukanda, specially. He leaps from the car when we get there, and off he runs! In the evening he presents himself to come back to Chomlaya, and he is very joyful! He does not tell me what it is about. He does not tell me who he speaks to. He says his friend Anna has some very good idea, but I do not know what he is talking about –'

'When did this happen?'

'Oi! Many days. Last week . . . Tuesday?'

'Who would know what it is about?'

The other spread his hands in a gesture of helplessness. 'I have asked Samuel; he knows nothing. We think this is a little secret these children are keeping. Inspector Murothi, I am truly sorry . . .'

'Likon, you have told me now, and that is well.' Murothi succeeded in speaking calmly; but his head reverberated with contradictory thoughts. He had been on his way to interrogate the teacher, Ian Boyd. Now, abruptly, he changed his mind.

'But you can give me some help, please. Sergeant Kaonga and the constables are busy wrestling the student books from Miss Strutton! But now let you and me go to speak to Silowa's cousin –'

'Mungai? He is here –'

'Yes, you will take me to find him, and help me in this conversation?'

They found him some little distance from the camp, with three other herdsmen, in the umbrella shade of an acacia. All sat facing the heights of Chomlaya, as if they kept watch. Their conversation was low-voiced, subdued. A bowl of food passed between them, their sticks leaned together against the tree, their long legs stretched in the dust.

At the approach of the inspector and Likon, they rose to their feet, together. Carefully they listened to Likon's greeting and introduction. In turn each took Murothi's proffered hand

and shook it, and Mungai looked hard at Murothi and spoke in his language that Murothi could not understand.

'Likon,' said Murothi. 'I am sorry, I do not have Mungai's language, and if Mungai does not have Kisewa . . .'

'Inspector, he has Kisewa, he travels far beyond his region. But of course I will help. Mungai is saying that he will stay till his young cousin is found. His family will expect this.'

Murothi nodded. He indicated the shade, and spoke carefully in Kisewa. 'Mungai, if you please, sit with me. I would like to understand something.'

A murmur passed between Mungai and his companions. They resumed their places below the tree. Murothi seated himself cross-legged in front of them and sifted the seeds of several ideas. 'I am told,' he began, 'that Silowa's home is far. That he came to this region with his uncle. That he stays away from his home. I am curious about this.'

'Silowa's uncle, yes. This is my father,' confirmed Mungai, this time in a form of Kisewa, heavily accented, that Murothi could nevertheless follow. 'Many times it is that my father goes to Burukanda. He brings news to the people there. He tells where he has seen the old bones lying, where the rain has washed the earth to show them. At Burukanda they are very interested in bones! This time, Silowa accompanies my father there. Silowa begs to –'

'He begs? Why does he do this?'

Elaborately, Mungai sighed. 'It is the stories. Always the stories. The boy listens to my father tell of Chomlaya, and before that, when he is small, he listens to his own father. This is in the years before the breathing illness took his father. But Silowa remembers. Many, many times, his father came to this place when he was a boy, together with my father – two boys very brave, very daring! His father tells how in days gone by, our ancestors came here when the time of their death call came. This lives in Silowa's head. He is restless . . .' Mungai swept his arm wide, encompassing the rock and the plain. 'When he has been to Burukanda and Chomlaya, and is again with his family, he wishes to return to Burukanda. Restless, always restless . . .'

'And the stories? They are of things that have happened here?'

'Tales told to children at their mother's knee. Of the beginnings of all things. It is said that the Creator leaves his footprints here. My father – you should hear him – he tells these things very well! And my young cousin, Silowa, at Burukanda he learns that another man, from a very far place, has a story about Chomlaya. It is like the stories of our fathers, but also different. Suddenly my cousin is buzzing like a bee! I do not know why it has this great enchantment for him. He is a very modern boy . . .' Mungai sucked his teeth and wrinkled his nose in an expression that was at once fond and despairing. 'Once he has been to Burukanda and Chomlaya he will not let anything rest! So his mother lets him come again, to try to find work and stay for some months. She hopes he will learn to let it go from his mind, and return to his home. Then,' he paused and indicated the student camp, 'what is troubling my thoughts, he meets these other young ones, and I do not know what has happened.' He shook his head: a slow, sad movement which drew murmurs from the others. Throughout they had been listening attentively to his account, nodding agreement here and there.

A sombre silence fell.

Gently, Murothi broke it. 'Perhaps he has just made good friends.'

The remark provoked one of the others, a young man, barely more than a boy himself. Rapidly he spoke in his own language in a tone that did not need translation for Murothi to recognise the annoyance.

Sympathetically, Likon glanced at Murothi. In English, he remarked, 'Inspector Murothi, they are afraid for Silowa. They do not like this running around these foreigners' camps.' He addressed them again in their own language and was quickly answered. To Murothi he explained, 'I ask if the uncle knows of Silowa's trouble here. I am told he is with the husbands of Silowa's sisters and the cattle, far, far,' he waved a hand towards the north. 'Mungai has sent a message with some who travel that way, but he does not know if it has reached them. To Silowa's mother as well, and his sisters.'

'I will find out if they know,' said Murothi. 'Promise him I will do this. The police have gone to find her, just as the English police are speaking to the mothers and fathers of the missing English children . . .'

Inexplicably, the statement chilled him. And where must *I* travel now? What trail must I follow? Bullying, bones, secrets, and now stories . . .

He thought, *Silowa feels called to these places, because his father, who is dead, walked these rocks; Silowa is perhaps no more than listening to the echoes.*

But in this there *is* something . . .

He saw the others had turned away and were observing a plume of dust rising like blood-red smoke above the scrub. There was a glint as sunlight caught glass, the thrum of an approaching engine. Now the vehicle was plainly in sight, bumping across the tussocky ground, slowing to a halt by the student camp. On the driver's side a lean, willowy, fair-haired woman flung open the door, got out and stretched arms above her head.

'It is Véronique,' said Likon, rising to his feet. 'Otaka will be with her. They are archaeologists from Burukanda. They are Charly's good friends.'

A tall African man emerged from the vehicle. He walked round the car and he and the woman went towards the camp. They could be seen speaking to a student. The student pointed towards Murothi.

The two visitors strode towards him.

'Inspector Murothi?' The woman's voice, strong, clear, unfamiliar in its accent, carried easily across the open ground. 'I am Véronique Mézard. If I may speak with you, please?'

'Véronique is French,' volunteered Likon, as if reading Murothi's mind.

'This is my friend and colleague, Otaka Ngolik,' the woman went on, drawing closer. 'We have been away. To the coast. We have read no newspapers, listened to no radios. A complete rest, we thought! We have only just received DC Meshami's message that he wishes to speak to us. We have come straightaway. We saw Charly, we want to tell you –'

Misunderstanding, Murothi's heart flipped.

'She is all right?'

'No, no, I do not mean that. If I understand matters correctly, it would be in the morning just *before* she went missing. She spent the previous day with us at Burukanda, and the night, and then she drove back to Chomlaya early. The thing is, Inspector, this may be important, she was so very happy about something. These pupils . . .' she gestured towards the camp.

'What something?'

She didn't answer directly, just turned and looked up at Chomlaya's jagged escarpments. 'Oh, I do not know, she did not tell me! Perhaps I talk nonsense! Perhaps she only came to talk, to send her email and collect her sister's. To get away from this camp, which more and more she did not like. She was content that these young friends of hers were going away for a few days – but I think she got this wrong? She believed they were going to Lengoi Springs.'

'She was not happy to leave them without her at the camp?'

'Well, she never said that. But yes, this is what I have come to think,' Véronique replied sombrely.

Until now, Otaka Ngolik had said nothing. At close range he was much older than the woman, his hair greyed, his manner calmly reserved. Now he commented, 'Charly came to show us something.'

'To show *you*, Otaka, my dear; she did not show me! And she swore *you* to secrecy! Inspector, Otaka has only just told me this, when we heard –'

'She showed you the sketchbook,' Otaka remarked, mildly, with a half-smile.

'Ah, yes, the drawings. Which she had taken from her young friend Anna because she feared this Miss Strutton would see them. They are very clever and very angry. Have you seen them, Inspector? But this was not the main thing she came for. She was checking the rules of the Burukanda competition –'

Murothi held up a hand. 'Competition? Please, please. I am drowning in competitions! I hear this word with every breath in this place! Explain this *Burukanda competition* . . .'

'It is called the Burukanda Award,' Véronique answered. 'It is for students, working in teams, to develop some original work. There is quite a lot of money in the prize, to be divided among the team. Charly wished to know if there was a restriction on who could enter. *And* who would be judging.'

'Is this the same competition the students here are working for now?'

'Now they work for it here,' Likon answered for Véronique.

'But before – Miss Strutton has the idea to make other little competitions, lots of little competitions, to select who will be *allowed* to enter the big Burukanda one!'

'Ah!' said Véronique emphatically. '*This* is what Charly hates. This nonsense! *This* is what she tries to stop! Competitions, competitions, competitions! Team points for this, team points for that! We were able to reassure her: the rules and the judgement of the Burukanda Award are in the hands of Burukanda only. The teachers at Chomlaya camp have no say. Charly felt that her young friends had a chance of making an interesting entry. But that was all she told us; she said this was not her secret to share.'

'I gave her a video camera,' Otaka put in. 'She could record whatever it was. She wished to ensure there was no doubt it was their work. She seemed very particularly worried about cheating or stealing.' He took something from his pocket. 'And she left this with me.'

From a small cloth pouch he tipped a fragment of something dark and brown, roughly triangular in shape, and held it flat on his hand for Murothi to see.

Murothi leaned forward to peer at it. It looked like a pebble.

'Part of a hominid skull. Fossilised,' explained the other

man. 'Here, you see, a little of the bony brow ridge. It is very prominent, thick, heavy. This suggests it is very, very early, but there is not enough to see properly. I do not know where Charly got this. She made me promise to tell no one else that I had it, not until she gave permission. I have not till now.' Otaka turned the fragment on the palm of his hand, contemplating it, then closed his fingers over it and slipped it back into the pouch. He looked meaningfully at Murothi. 'If these children found anything like this near Chomlaya, it would be thrilling, it would be very, very clever of them . . . to find it, and to *know* what it is.'

'Come,' broke in Véronique. 'Ride out with us, Inspector. Likon, my friend, you too.' Briskly she blocked Murothi's hesitation: 'It will not take long. It may reveal something about these children's preoccupations that you have not considered. It is only necessary to go a little way out . . .'

They stood on an outcrop of rock. It rose to the height of a tree, its top worn by wind and water to a broad platform curved like a shallow dish. Véronique, Otaka and Likon had climbed effortlessly, finding toeholds and fingerholds invisible to Murothi, who scrambled and slithered and arrived at the top puffing, fingersore and hot.

'There you see it: an archaeologist's nightmare. A geologist's nightmare!' declared Véronique.

The full sweep of the land was revealed, its gradual fall northwards towards the long, snaking spine of rock that was Chomlaya. To their left, at its western end, the fractured and fissured dying line of the ridge was visible as the occasional jagged barb speared upward through the earth. At the eastern end, to the right of the student camp, the huge bulbous formations of reddish rock seemed to Murothi like a vast head, half-turned to look at him, resting in the afternoon sunshine.

'You may see now,' murmured Otaka, considering it through binoculars, 'why for some it is known as Snake Rock.'

'And why do you say it is a nightmare?' enquired Murothi.

'Do you know anything about rocks, Inspector?' was Véronique's reply.

'Nothing.'

'With Chomlaya, it is impossible to unpick the course of its life. There is a volcanic core spewed upwards in multiple eruptions many millennia ago. But on this there are deposits of other rocks, formed from sediments swept here by wind and water over millions more years. None of this is unusual, of course. But what makes it so difficult to understand is that it has been ruptured again and again by more recent volcanic activity.

It has split, buckled, twisted. Everything is topsy-turvy, up and down and round each other, jostled and tilted. And then it is confused even more by recent soil movements. We expect caves, but there are none. But the real point is this, Inspector: there has never been any serious exploration of it. Over the years, everyone has circled warily round about; we snoop to the west and east and south, but never at Chomlaya's feet —'

Otaka put a hand on her shoulder. 'My friends, something happens!' Quickly he passed the binoculars to Murothi.

Beyond Chomlaya, the dark insect shape of a helicopter was rising, circling, dipping again. And from the trees shrouding the camp, three figures could be seen running forward on to the open ground where the Land Rover had parked only half an hour before. And what Otaka had seen, and what Murothi saw now, was that all three were waving. Something white, in long high sweeps. Signalling and signalling and signalling. As though somebody's life depended on it.

3 p.m.

'It's Matt, Matt, Matt!' Joe was yelling, careering in a demented jig round the Land Rover as it slewed to a halt, and swinging a laughing Ella with him. 'I heard him, I heard him, I heard him . . .' and the two of them plunged back into a knot of jubilant students.

At sight of Murothi, Constable Lesakon rushed towards him. 'Sir, you have seen us signal! We hoped you will see us!'

'What does Joe mean? Are they found?'

'Ah, no! Just Matt,' emphatically the constable shook his head. 'The helicopter, just now, it sees him. He lies on the ground. Now the helicopter will lift him up, and they will go to the hospital.'

'The others?'

'No, Sir. No one else.'

Murothi breathed deep, relief and disappointment warring in equal measure. He climbed out of the vehicle. 'And what does Joe mean – this *I heard him?*'

The constable waggled his head and looked at Samuel for help.

'The boy thinks he heard Matt play the pipe.' Samuel sighed. 'Inspector, it cannot be so. Matt is unconscious. It is true that he clutches a pipe – the pilots have told us this. But Matt is very weak! How can he play this pipe and be heard here? It is more than two miles away! Across the rock? It is impossible. Joe has heard a bird! Or it is the voice of hope in our young friend; I see this.'

'This may be true, Samuel.' Murothi slammed the vehicle door and moved towards the milling crowd, scanning for the sergeant. He took in the presence of Ian Boyd, the other teachers. And Miss Strutton. She stood to one side.

'Constable Lesakon, do we know if the climbers are still on the rock?'

'Sergeant Kaonga tries to reach them on the radio – the reception is very troublesome. But he has talked to DC Meshami in Nanzakoto. The DC is very happy! He has ordered a repeat search of all . . .' He flung his arms wide, denoting the length and breadth of Chomlaya. 'We will discover these others!'

'And Matt was found where Joe was found?'

'Ah, no – it is on the top, a mile away. And it is that way. That is why we search all over there again.' The constable pointed to their right along the rock, beyond the camp, beyond the dark cross-cut of the ravine, etched hard in deepening afternoon shadow.

That stopped Murothi in his tracks. He pondered the information. One boy near the bottom of the northern cliffs of Chomlaya, coming down the gully of a dried-up river. The other, three days later, on its summit. Neither one on *this* side, on the southern face that might be reached direct from the camp.

It made no sense.

'And, Sir, I have this,' continued the constable. 'Joe and the clever little sister of the journalist, they find them for us.' He took a bundle from under his arm and presented it proudly to Murothi. 'It is the journalist's writings, Sir, and –'

'Oh!' interrupted Véronique, starting forward. 'That is Anna's sketchbook, the one Charly showed to me – I told you, Inspector!'

Murothi took the books. He did not open them. His mind fizzed. He struggled to think calmly. The hullabaloo from the students was infectious. He wanted to dance with Joe and Ella. He wanted to leap up the cliff and find Charly and Anna and Silowa, now, this minute, alive and well . . .

'It will be night.' Across the clamour of voices, Mungai's deep, unhurried tones floated clearly. He was standing nearby, his eyes ranging backwards and forwards along the rock. 'If two are there, it is that all are there.' He gestured to the lengthening shadows, the already dipping sun in the west. 'But night will come.'

'Mungai, they can go on with these big helicopters,' Samuel told him. 'It is the army. They have giant lights.'

'Inspector, Otaka and I will stay for the night,' Véronique announced briskly. 'We will help in whatever way we can. Now you are busy. We talk later?'

They did not wait for an answer, climbing into the Land Rover, rattling some way across the bumpy ground before stopping. Among the low scrubby bushes, the battered old vehicle merged like the tired brown hulk of an animal settling for the night.

Sergeant Kaonga's words tumbled out in excitement: 'In a few minutes the helicopter will depart with Matt. The DC will receive him in Nanzakoto, and go to the hospital with him. There will be someone with good English with Matt through all the night. We will know *the moment* he wakes up, Sir. Straightaway! We must remain here. We must encourage Joe. It is very odd that he says he hears something and then the same moment the helicopter soldiers call us! It is very surprising!

I think this boy has these things hidden just here,' he tapped his forehead, 'just wanting to come out! This talking, this walking about, it is all helping! It is hopeful now! But we must be quick, *quick* to find the others . . .'

Murothi was watching Joe and Ella, surrounded by Tamara, Janey, Zak and Antony. Everyone was talking exuberantly. He imagined Matt, as he had first seen Joe, bruised and battered in the hospital. Matt would be weaker than Joe, because three more days had passed. But perhaps with memories, knowledge . . . *It is hopeful. It is, it is.*

Beyond the students, Miss Strutton turned away. Murothi saw she had not entered into the jubilation, merely watched, without expression. Noting the direction of the inspector's gaze, the sergeant remarked, 'I have to report, Sir, I fail to get these student writings. She says they are "not important . . . you have no right . . . it is an invasion of our privacy."'

It was a clever mimicry of the teacher's tart tones, and Murothi could not help a smile. 'We could instruct her. But it is a false trail, I think, and there is nothing there that we should not freely see. I am sorry to make you waste your time.'

'She says no, because it is in her nature to say no,' commented Samuel darkly. 'She becomes a teacher because children are smaller than her, and she can say *no* more often.'

This time Murothi laughed, and the constable laughed, and the sergeant clapped Samuel on the shoulder, the relief at Matt's rescue, all the renewed hope it brought, becoming for that moment an interlude from serious business. It was interrupted only by the teacher, Ian Boyd, appearing suddenly in their midst.

'Inspector, Sergeant, anything I can do – we can do – the teachers, I mean? Or the students?'

'Ah,' Murothi blurted, 'you are the first teacher of these missing children to ask!'

The man flushed deep red, and looked away. And Murothi wished he had kept his mouth shut: now a door that *had* been opening would be slammed shut again. But then Ian Boyd volunteered, 'Yes . . . well, point taken, Inspector. Miss Strutton insisted she must handle everything. Everyone else to stay away and not *confuse* matters.' He cleared his throat. 'With what's at stake, that is plainly ridiculous.'

'I do not mean to be impolite,' Murothi apologised. 'To tell you the truth, Mr Boyd, I have been told that you have frequent disagreements with Miss Strutton.'

A frown creased Ian Boyd's face. 'Well . . . difficult to explain. Some teachers measure intelligence by how well the tasks they give are performed. Curiosity, exploration, initiative, experiment – they see these as indiscipline and disobedience.'

'Are you saying Miss Strutton is like that?'

'She'd probably be shocked if you said that to her, but, yes, that's the *effect*. The thing is, normally I wouldn't challenge another teacher in front of students. Certainly not in these circumstances, when running the camp with clear lines of authority is so important. Safety – all that – don't need to explain it to you, I'm sure, Inspector.'

The teacher stared away, and Murothi had the impression he was not going to say more. But he suddenly switched his gaze firmly back. 'If you can imagine, these weeks here are to encourage the students to be curious about things beyond themselves – to look outward. That's what we *meant* it to be: Helen and Keith and me. That's why we contacted Charly, to get her to document the experience for her magazine.'

'And . . .?' urged Murothi, because to his immense frustration, Ian Boyd had fallen silent again.

'It's also meant to be about fostering team work, *real* team work. Team spirit. Leadership. That's the *theory*. Trouble is, in our leader's mind "team spirit" is "competitiveness".' He laughed sourly. 'And leadership means, "I'm right, you're wrong, don't argue!"'

'We all get a dose of this medicine,' Murothi observed drily, and the teacher gave him a direct look, almost of relief.

'Well, Elisa Strutton's a Deputy Head of the school – one of three – it's a big school. Headteacher puts her in charge of this trip to Africa – bingo, she's not one of three any more! Big fish, small pond –' He caught sight of the books in Murothi's hands. 'Anna's book!' he exclaimed. 'I thought it was lost.'

'Why?'

'Oh – Anna said she didn't have it when we collected them in.'

'It will be instructive?'

'I haven't seen what's in it. But maybe. You probably should know Anna is a casualty of resisting Miss Strutton.'

'Explain.'

'Oh, well, not much to say. Miss Strutton teaches technology. Last term she humiliated a boy whose work wasn't very good. Threw some piece into the corner, so it smashed, couldn't be marked. Anna objected, complained to the head of year. Fireworks! Now Anna's A Class One Troublemaker. Elisa even opposed her coming here . . .' A horrified expression came over his face. 'You don't think it has anything to do with their disappearance, do you? I *really* don't –'

'No, Mr Boyd, not directly. But I need to understand the "mood" here. I find it strange. You are not able to influence it?'

'Well . . .' Discomfort was now visible in a shift of stance and hunching of Ian Boyd's shoulders. 'Elisa's difficult to persuade, even at the best of times! Here, you get a backlash, when you're not looking. Usually against one of the students. Makes you pull your punches, if you see what I mean. Anyway, arguments about the way the camp is run, too often a bit public . . . not good for general morale . . .'

This man has run away from the problem, thought Murothi. *And he knows it, and now he is ashamed.*

There was a sudden throaty roar, and from beyond the ridge a helicopter cleared the summit in an ear-splitting acceleration. It veered across the camp, the chop of its blades deafening, swirling dust into miniature tornados. It zigzagged in a final jaunty signal which raised a cheer from the watchers. Then it swung away, setting course towards the south-west and the hospital at Nanzakoto. Rapidly it dwindled to a tiny black speck in the sky.

From the north-east a distant droning became steadily stronger. Within minutes two new helicopters could be detected heading towards them, growing larger and larger by the minute.

'I really just wanted to say,' asserted Ian Boyd, 'we're here, if you need us for anything . . .'

'It will be a long afternoon, perhaps a long night, Mr Boyd, while these searches continue. We look for anything, anything that will help direct the helicopters. We wait and hope for information from Matt. We try to help Joe's mind to open a little more.' Murothi found himself looking up at Chomlaya. 'We look for help from any quarter it comes.'

nightfall

'What's happening?' asked Tamara. 'We thought maybe something more's happened.' She came further under the awning of Ella's tent, into the light of the paraffin lamp.

'They just heard from the hospital,' said Ella. 'They're rehydrating Matt, but he's very weak, and he's still not conscious. And Sergeant Kaonga's spoken on the radio to the helicopters too. He says they'll be going all night, and he promises to say if anything happens.'

'Oh. OK.' The other girl looked round curiously, unwilling to go. 'Where's Joe?'

'There.'

He sat a little way out, watching the darkness, the shadow of a herd moving beyond the ring of yellow thrown by the powerful camp lamps. If you stared hard enough you caught the curve of an antler, the gleam of a zebra's stripe, and Ella could almost believe she heard the tearing of grass, the shuffle and knock of hooves on beaten ground. The moon was rising, hard and bright in a clear sky, and with it, as if drawn from the earth by the moon's climb, the chorus of crickets and frogs.

Joe didn't move at Tamara's enquiry. He was cross-legged, elbows on his knees, hands plucking absent-mindedly at spiky grass.

Tamara gazed at him for a minute. 'You should come to the fire, Ella. You and Joe. We're all there. You should come.'

Ella looked across at the inspector's tent. No light inside: he wasn't back from the police tents. Nine hours till first light. The night stretched, long and dark, ahead.

'Joe, let's go,' she urged.

As if returning from somewhere, he looked at her. But at once he leapt up. Since nightfall, the heady exhilaration at Matt's rescue five hours ago had given way to a jumpy, fretful edginess. He needed something to do, like she did. To ward off unbearable pictures that sneaked in whenever she let her mind fall idle.

A scatter of loose groups spread around the central space. Some played cards under the canteen canopy where lamps reflected strongly off the white canvas. Most sprawled round the fire, and there was an immediate general shuffling to make room for Joe and Ella. Tamara gave a few quick introductions for Ella: people smiled, a hand raised here and there in greeting, but nothing was said, directly. Conversations carried on, punctuated only by a yelp and nervous laughter as bats sped low across their heads and into the night.

The darkness crowded in, a thousand eyes glittering in the firelight. She could hear, too, the insistent throb of the helicopters on the other side of Chomlaya, though it was dulled by the height of the rocks and split by the spasmodic screams of hyrax. Then from somewhere behind, she heard, 'No, but it *is*. It's like that time, in that film, when these people disappear on a rock and they never find them!'

'Don't say that! Don't say *never*!'

'I saw that film – *Picnic at Hanging Rock*. My sister's got it.'

'Wait, wait, it's not the same – we'll find them!'

'It's a *story*, that *Picnic* film.'

'No, it's true!'

'Not! It's a story – from a book, I saw about it on the internet.'

'Well, Matt and Joe have come back already, so the others –'

A loud laugh stemmed the flow. Ella, already jarred by the talk and now by the laugh – strident, scornful, meant to be heard, meant to *interrupt* – swung round to see who it was.

The girls discussing the film sat a little way off. At Ella's glance, realising she'd overheard, one flicked her an apologetic glance. The others were glaring, annoyed, towards people sitting away from the fire. It took just a brief survey for Ella to detect the laugher: Sean, propped on one elbow, cards splayed in his hand. But his mind was not on the card game. His eyes scoured everyone near the fire, coming to rest first on Joe, and then on Ella.

Ella looked away.

At her side, Tamara said, 'You stay clear of him.' She was looking at Sean.

'What's going on with him, anyway?' Ella asked. 'What's he got to do with Joe?'

Tamara looked down. There was a long, disquieting silence, and Ella had the impression that now everyone was listening, except perhaps Joe, who just plucked at the grass in a maddening, restless twitch.

'Dunno,' Tamara muttered finally. 'Dunno what Sean's got to do with anything . . . You stay clear of him though. Hear what I'm saying?'

'He thinks he's bad,' put in Janey. 'You know, thinks he's really bad. Thinks he can do anything.'

'Well, he came to Joe's tent . . .' began Ella.

Joe's head snapped up.

'When you were sleeping,' she said. 'You know, before . . .'

'You should've said!'

'It was OK. I just want to know why . . .'

'You know what?' Janey broke in. 'At school he wasn't this way. He's something else, now. Sean. It's that Strutton. Her and all that. I tell you, here, he thinks no one'll say no to him any more. Ella should just stay clear, that's right, hey, Joe?'

Joe wasn't hearing. Around him, others peopled the night – another night, not so long ago: Silowa walking from the dark into firelight and Anna shrieking, *Silowa, don't spook me! Don't do that!* Silowa chuckling, holding the bundle out, *Matt, my good friend, I will make a presentation to you,* and Matt unrolling the cloth, the reed lying, gleaming, slender, burnished by the fireglow . . . Matt's face splitting ear to ear with a grin; he lifts it, fingers the holes, blows a soft, whispery note, takes a breath and blows again – the note thin, building, opening, swelling, singing suddenly on the full high note of a bird; Silowa folding his long bony legs and sitting down beside him, *It is my friend Ndigi that has made it for you! He will come tomorrow to hear you play it!*

So who cares now if that Strutton-monster's got the harmonica? Anna drapes an arm over Matt's shoulder as the trills run up and down, up and down, higher and higher, and then finally down again to a deep, belling note, and a smattering of clapping from someone across the fire and a shout, 'Play something proper, Matt. Play that –'

Hey! Hey, you!

The tone unmistakable.

I said YOU.

Silence: like an avalanche of ice.

Yes, YOU. Whad'you want?

I do not understand.

Silowa, ignore him, says Joe.

Don't understand English, hey? I said, whad'you want?

Shut up, Sean, says Anna.

I visit my friends, says Silowa.

Go visit them somewhere else.

Sean! Zak's protest vehement. But snapped off by the way Sean turns and looks at him, and then at Antony. Who says nothing . . .

'Sorry, Joe. Really. Sorry.' Janey's voice penetrated the memory, and she was leaning towards him, insistent, as if she saw what was in his head.

'We should have, y'know . . .' said Antony.

Zak grunted.

'What are you on about?' asked Ella. 'What are they on about, Joe?'

No one told her, just stared fixedly at the fire, every one of them. Then someone dropped more wood on it, and it snapped and popped and threw up a volley of angry sparks. Out on the plain, the eyes shifted, pinpricks of flame in the dark.

'Stuff,' said Joe suddenly, 'just stuff.'

'*Tell* me,' Ella insisted.

He didn't.

'Joe?'

He gave a small shrug.

'You're not being fair!' she said hotly. 'This is about my sister, too.'

He glanced at her in surprise. Flushed with indignation, the glare she gave him stung. He conceded, 'Stupid things. People picked on us. Not important now.'

'Sean?'

'Him. He had a few helpers.'

'Like *who*, Joe? What did they do? How do you know it's not important if you can't remember anything?'

That struck home, because he still couldn't drag sense from this chaos — fractured and nonsensical, blurred and muddled, memory and dream twisted together, frightening him more than he cared to admit.

Trying, he began, 'Like – going on and on at Silowa about

being here; Anna and me and Matt about hanging out with him. Like falling about being buffalos blundering through the tents in the night so they'd collapse on us. Like tipping Matt in the lavatory trench, slinging his pipe after him. Flat on his face. He has to wade through the filth to find his pipe. Never got the smell off his shoes, so Strutton throws everything out of the tent because she says it stinks like a toilet!' He stared away into the dark ferociously. 'Like Strutton banning us from the trips. Making us dig the new lavatory trenches after the storm because that mob told her we had "an outsider" in our tent, and it was a "breach of security". Like chucking Anna and Silowa's fossils because it was a "breach of hygiene".' He snorted. 'Like I said, he had some helpers –'

'They did the scorpion,' said Tamara, igniting the image in Joe's head – the two girls tittering, Joe pushing past, ripping open the zip, freezing at the sight of Anna rooted to the bed; the scorpion a finger's-width from her eyes, tail poised to strike, so that he had to edge back, grab a stick and advance again, stick extended, inch by slow inch, till he was in range and could knock the scorpion away.

And finding it dead, dead all the time, but Anna had been trapped for an hour, suspended in terror, while two girls spied and giggled at the joke.

'Didn't you tell anyone? You could tell *someone*. Someone could *do* something,' Ella was saying.

'There's always comeback after,' insisted Tamara.

'Nowhere to go, here –'

'Anyway, it got worse. It's getting worse. That's what I'm seeing,' came a boy's voice from the other side of the fire. 'Starts off stupid – baby stuff. Gets bigger. You have to keep away. So they don't *see* you, know what I mean?'

'But who's in Anna's tent? I mean sharing with her? Didn't they help?'

'What, those two?' Joe flung his arm out, pointing, and Ella looked. They sat close to Sean, one girl plaiting the other's hair as she leaned against his legs. With a jolt of comprehension, Ella recognised the two who had confronted her after breakfast.

'Them? She shared with them? How come?'

'Who knows? Miss wouldn't move her to our tent,' said Janey. 'We had space. Miss said Anna joined the trip late, so she's got to take what she gets.'

'So they got their kicks out of zipping up the tent from inside and not letting her in, "finding" hairy spiders in her sleeping bag . . .'

'Yeah, and sniggering about Silowa. Called him her *boyfriend*,' said Tamara, mimicking a suggestive drawl. 'Can't get their heads round things like being *friends*,' she finished, contemptuously.

But the carcass, dripping. The blood and stench of the carcass. That was something new. For a split second something else lurched at the back of Joe's mind, and his stomach leapt in a surge of fright.

'But why you, Joe?' Ella's interrogation stabbed through.

'*I* don't know what gets them going!'

'But you see, Silowa's an *outsider*!' Zak jumped to his feet and mimicked Strutton's voice and walk with such accuracy that, despite themselves, everyone laughed, even Ella.

'Right, and Matt's so *small* –'

'And Anna's A *Troublemaker* –'

'And Joe's their *protector*.'

Ella felt Joe tense. There was a silence.

'Didn't though, did I?' he muttered after a minute. '*Didn't*.' He was quiet for a minute. He began again. 'It was like it before Silowa came. Just got more – *obvious* – after.'

'Policeman said, we do nothing, they'll die,' commented Zak soberly. 'Can't walk away now. Can't say don't want no trouble now.'

They all contemplated this.

'It's true what they say, Joe – you don't remember anything

about going out of the camp?' Antony asked. 'How come?'

'Leave it, Ant,' Zak protested. 'You sound like the police. Interrogating and that.'

'No, but is it true? You heard Matt's pipe?'

'Thought I did,' said Joe. 'But it's too far. They say.'

'Those two,' announced Antony suddenly, looking at Carl and Denny, sauntering away, 'are just thugs. They were before. But *Sean's* a predator. He's testing out his hunting ground.'

'Oh, *deep*,' said Janey.

'But, see, predators, real ones like the animals out there, they do it so they can live, if they didn't they'd *die* –'

'But what's it got to do with everyone disappearing?' Suddenly Ella wanted to yell with frustration.

Joe looked at her, lifting his shoulders in a gesture of despair, and his face took on that stricken look she'd seen before.

And as if to echo him, a helicopter suddenly topped the ridge, its searchlight arcing across the rock and raking the camp. And then it sank away, out of sight, only its engine-grumble lingering. As if to fill the returning quiet, the distant roar of a lion swelled from the darkness of the plain.

'Remember Matt when he heard a lion that first night?' said Janey. 'It was like Christmas for him! Went on about it all day. Remember?'

'Wish they'd let us see him,' said Zak. 'Before they took him off. Wish we could've talked . . .'

Otaka sat by the small fire, smoking. He raised his pipe in greeting to Murothi. From above, Véronique peered from the roof of the Land Rover. She was kneeling, spreading something out.

'Inspector! Join us – we would be happy,' she called. 'I am just arranging my bedroom!' She clambered down a ladder and pointed to a canvas stool by the fire. 'Sit!'

Murothi obeyed. Since nightfall the temperature had plunged, and in his thin shirt, damped with dew, he shivered. He watched Véronique throw back the lid of a food box and rattle things busily.

Otaka, with a long, direct scrutiny of the policeman, observed, 'My friend, you are troubled.'

'Ah, well, you see a confused Murothi,' the policeman responded. 'And his confusion grows!'

Véronique placed a pot in the fire and settled it firmly. She fetched another stool from the Land Rover, flipped it open and subsided on to it, thankfully.

Otaka continued to puff on his pipe. Then he took it from

his mouth and with the stem traced the long ridge of Chomlaya, fringed with the light of the climbing moon. He said, 'It is told by the Dumwela people that this is the seat of the God. That he lives here as rock, as elephant, as snake, as fish in the water, as lion, as lizard, as hare. He is in the bones of the rock and the gouging of the rift through its heart . . .'

'Old friend, you would know that,' said Véronique, handing Murothi a mug of steaming tea and a biscuit. 'You have studied the line of this land as no other person living.'

'But I do not breathe it, like the men who walk it,' replied Otaka. 'I do not hear the call of ancestors.' He laughed. 'I fear in my old age I will be like those polished men in fat black cars that fly above the land on shiny roads, and do not touch it.'

'I have met those,' said Murothi, thinking of the Minister who had sent him to tidy away this disaster. The tea was warming him. He had eaten little; hunger hollowed out his tiredness. His eyes seemed to stand out on stalks, but he did not want to go to the solitude of his tent and the muddles of his mind.

As if sensing that, Véronique refilled his mug. 'Perhaps such stories of Chomlaya are why we have never come to dig here. As if we believe them, and are afraid.'

'Silowa's cousin Mungai has told me of these tales,'

said Murothi, sipping the tea.

'Mungai is not of the Dumwela. He is of the Kigio,' murmured Otaka. 'The Kigio have a story that is like the story told by the Dumwela, but it is not the same.' Thoughtfully, he puffed on his pipe. 'Some do not call this place by any other name than Snake Rock. But others tell how when the God enters his human form he leaves his footprint here. To guard the place where the first people were born. It is like this, my friend: there came a day when the Creator looked at the trees and flowers, the mountains and rivers, the animals and birds – at every good thing he had made – and he said, "There must be a creature to love and tend this, to reap its riches." So the Creator took the soils he found at Chomlaya's feet: the rich moist soils, the soft powdery soils, the black soils, red soils, white soils, yellow soils. He took some of each and mixed it to a clay, and from the wealth of clays he made people of all the colours. He moulded legs to run, to hunt, to wander with the cattle and dance for joy, hands to gather food, to plant and sow, and reap, he gave eyes to see, a mouth to eat, a tongue to speak and sing, for people would need celebration when the work was done . . .' He gave Murothi a long, sober look. 'You see this: it is told that in the shelter of Chomlaya, the Creator has made humans. It is the place of life. And here he calls his creatures

216

when their time is done; the place of life, the place of death. For these children, their time of calling is not yet here. And so Chomlaya will give them back. This we must *believe*.' He straightened suddenly, smiled, lightening the mood, tapped his pipe and relit it, puffing hard. 'Tales told in many ways by many different peoples in these regions. But we should hear them and take heart, my friend.'

Long fingers of firelight probed grass and bush and the cones of termite mounds around them. There was the guttural grunt of a leopard hunting, the scuffle of hoofbeats as something fled the predator, and Murothi wondered if he should feel fear here: of the rock that might be a god, and the leopard and lion that might be a god, and the rock that had taken people but would give them back, and he felt foolish for breathing these stories that were just stories into himself.

In truth he did not feel fear. He felt Chomlaya hunched above them, black against a high yellow moon. But his dread was not of the rock.

He said, after a while, 'I have a question. I have many questions, but this is one you can perhaps answer. Likon says that a week ago Silowa came to talk to someone at Burukanda, specially. Otaka, was that you?'

'Silowa is always talking to me,' the other man answered,

with a deep chuckle of amusement. 'He has appointed himself my pupil. He wishes to learn this skill of fossil hunting.'

'Silowa is already like you,' put in Véronique. 'He lopes across the ground like you. He has your eye for these invisible things! Otaka and Silowa see a single tiny fossil among the black lava pebbles on a slope. They see fossils that not one other person would see! They conjure them from the ground as they pass, Inspector!'

'*Murothi*,' said Murothi. 'I am Murothi. I do not know this Inspector! He is quite new to me.'

Véronique raised her mug of tea in salute.

'You are right,' remarked Otaka pensively. 'Silowa came to me some days ago. I think this is the time Likon is meaning. I remember that the boy wanted to know about tuffs.'

'Tuffs? What are these?'

'Layers of volcanic ash, compacted to rock,' offered Véronique. 'Murothi, think of a volcano spewing out the ash. Or the volcanic ash carried far by rivers and dumped. In the heat and pressure of volcanic eruption, there are changes in the minerals –'

'I do not understand,' protested Murothi, already lost.

'It sets a kind of atomic clock going, which we can use to tell when the eruption happened. So, we date the tuffs! If we find something trapped below a tuff, it is older, if it is above a tuff, it is younger. Of course, sometimes things have been twisted upside down, as in Chomlaya, making it difficult to trace the line of the tuffs from one place to another. Is the archaeological find really above or below? Has some great rift in the earth flung everything on its head? I tell you, we can go quietly mad with this!'

'And this enquiry about tuffs. This is the kind of question Silowa would usually ask? Did this talk seem different?'

Emphatically, Otaka shook his head. 'This boy is always eager. He drinks knowledge like it is the water of life. We have many of these conversations while we work.'

Murothi, sipping his third cup of tea, could think of nothing else to ask. Whispers seemed to float in and out of his head. It is the tiredness, he thought. He passed a hand across his face, pressing his eyes. *It is sleep that calls –*

'You have the face of a haunted man,' commented Otaka, getting up and fetching sticks, placing them on the fire, sitting down again and studying Murothi.

'I *am* haunted, Otaka. These voices haunt me.' Murothi waved a hand at the little pile at his feet, shining pale against the soil. He leaned down and picked it up. 'Here, you see, Anna's drawings and your friend Charly's notes. Then we have these police interviews, the students' camp diary, Charly's emails and letters to Ella. I have what the students have said, and what Joe has told me. I have talked and talked to Joe since Matt was found. I have the voice of his distress that he does not know the answers. I have Ella who *knows* her sister.' He sighed. 'And now I have your voices too! Ah! They all tell different stories and I know, in here,' he tapped his head, 'that they are the same story. But I cannot see the joining points.'

deep night

Ella struggled free of the sleeping bag and flopped on top. Sweat dried, sticky on her skin.

There was a slight, furtive, rasping sound. It came to her at the same moment she saw a change in the light through the canvas. With a flip of alarm, she knew that someone stood there.

Not Joe. Too tall.

She sat up, swinging her legs to the ground. The zip was opening, a figure slipping deftly through the gap.

'Who –?'

'*Shut up.*'

He came on silently and fast, reached the bed and stood over her, legs wide, her knees trapped between his, close, pressing.

She pushed, trying to twist from his hold, throw herself sideways. But he held her effortlessly by the shoulder, one hand pressing her down, the grip painful, his other hand groping for her mouth.

'Wha–?' she mumbled, frantic to think straight.

'Dunno,' he said. 'Makes it interesting?'

'*Get out.*' Joe was a square of black against the opening, without form or feature, except his voice.

'You'll make me?'

'Yes.'

Sean laughed. 'How?'

'Don't know. But I will . . .'

'Well, won't wait while you figure it out.' He shoved Ella's shoulder spitefully. It flung her against the metal edge of the camp-bed with a bang that drew a yelp of pain, and instantly Joe launched himself, toppling Sean sideways over Ella's backpack on the floor.

Expertly the taller boy rolled to his feet and dived at Joe, the whole taking place in a muted, grunting fury: thud, thump against the ground, hoarse, strangled breaths, Ella tumbling with them, scrabbling to hold Sean, weigh him down, drag him off. *Fetch someone* pounded through her brain even as running feet and torchbeams split the dark. Boys' voices, girls' . . . Miss Strutton's bark, '*Where DO you think you're going?*'

'He came here, Miss. He's –'

'*Back to your tents this minute.*'

'– looking for Sean, Miss –'

'*How DARE you run about like this? You know the rules!*'

'Yeah, but *he's* not meant to be out, either –'

'*I'll be the judge of that!*'

'We saw Sean come this way –'

'*Since when is that your business?*'

'Since *now*, Miss. We got to find what Sean's doing!'

Then everyone silenced as Ella pulled the tent flap wide and stumbled out.

It took seconds – the two wrestling boys tugged apart, Sean kneeling viciously on Joe as he got up, aiming a last vindictive kick. 'Later,' he muttered. To Ella, not Joe. He shouldered past her, shrugged everyone else off and flung away, hurling a glance of open scorn at the dumbstruck Miss Strutton.

For a moment there was a startled vacuum, as if no one had really expected to find anything happening. And then the inspector and the sergeant coming at a run from the police tents, and the teacher Ian Boyd from somewhere else, and a general babble of explanation.

Suddenly shivery, sapped, Ella turned back into the tent. Joe was sitting on the camp-bed. He gave her a shaky smile. She sat down beside him.

'Right,' she could hear Ian Boyd saying outside. 'Good, everyone. Now, back to your tents. No random wandering about with the main lamps out. Don't want surprise encounters with other kinds of wildlife. Get some sleep now. Need you all fit and alert tomorrow. Inspector Murothi, I'll see to Joe and Ella. And we'll look for Sean, find out what he thinks he's up to. We'll keep an eye on him – Oi, you lot, don't take liberties! Off you go.'

Zak's head came poking into the tent, followed by Antony and Tamara: like a totem pole, their faces one below the other. Zak gave a thumbs-up, and the others grinned, and then they withdrew into the sounds of general chatter, voices and footsteps gradually drifting away.

After a minute, Ian Boyd peered in. Then he came fully inside, shone a torch over Ella's face and then Joe's, examining carefully.

'Hurt?'

Ella, tears of delayed fear and shock welling up, shook her head dumbly.

'Sure?'

She nodded.

'Joe?'

'He's a savage, Sir, he's a –'

'And you stopped him, Joe. That's more than . . .' the teacher hunched his shoulders, didn't complete the sentence.

'Look, get some rest – both of you. Stuff to do as soon as it's light. Won't be long, now. I'll be keeping watch. We'll sort Sean out. Promise.' He glanced from one to the other, seemed on the point of saying something else, and didn't. He went out.

'He'll come back,' said Ella. She meant Sean.

'Maybe,' said Joe. 'Yeah, he'll try.' He put his arm round her shoulder, pulled her against him and sat holding her. 'I'll stay. Two of us?'

Outside, all the torchlight had gone. Only a sliver of moonlight slipped across the groundsheet.

Suddenly Joe got up, zipped up the tent, and moved Ella's pack against the entrance.

'Trip him up,' he said. 'Warn us. We got to sleep. Like Sir said. It'll be light soon.'

He climbed on to the camp-bed beside her, put his arm across her and pushed her down, gently. He settled, and shut his eyes.

For a while she studied his face, a shadowy mosaic of contours in the dark, until her shiveriness ebbed away. Then she turned over, pushed up close to him so she could feel his warmth against her back, and went to sleep.

The notebook slid off Murothi's chest and fell to the groundsheet with a slap. The lamp guttered, burning low and yellow.

Something had jolted him awake. Something rattled in his head.

It is two separate events. These people have left the camp for one reason. They have disappeared for another. In these *two* things is the answer; Murothi, do not confuse their *separateness.*

Dawn was still two hours away. His throat was dry. He heaved himself off the bed and found his water bottle, drank thirstily. The liquid coursed through him, cooling, kindling him to an alert wakefulness.

He picked up the fallen notebook. On the cover Charly had written CHOMLAYA CAMP/ OPENED 6 FEBRUARY 2006. Twenty-three days ago.

What had struck him most was its scale and care: dated, meticulous, detailed. Notes about the place: sketchmaps, plants, animals, birds; trips made with students; notes of conversations with them: families, interests, friends. Likon, Tomis, Samuel – they were all there, and the two drivers, David Ntanyaki and Nicolas Waiputari. Even the various English teachers. She seemed to have made a point of talking, carefully, to everyone. There were Otaka and Véronique; other names from Burukanda that Murothi did not know. And all this was interspersed with her impressions, reactions, thoughts – even quotations. Like one from Samuel: *He who is unable to dance says the yard is stony.* Murothi could not help smiling, having a very good idea that the 'he' in this case was probably a 'she', Miss Strutton.

He thought, you can trace the course of Charly's mood, day by day. Here, in that first week, is her elation: Chomlaya, her happiness that the students were so enthusiastic, new sights, new friends. Barely two weeks later, is the beginning of the descent . . .

The first hint came in a note on 18 February.

You can see what's happened – this friend of Ian's comes here, falls in love with it – inspires Ian to organise the trip, he gets me involved, we all share an idea about why we've come . . .

CRASH, bad fairy lands at the party: I'M IN CHARGE!

It's a personal kingdom for ES – not thirty kids and a handful of teachers in a semi-desert place, a place they DON'T KNOW, which could turn against them in a flash.

She's got to decide everything. Disagree with her, and it's I DON'T HAVE TIME FOR THIS. She SULKS, she FUMES (if there were doors to slam, she'd slam them). The most ridiculous, tiniest detail of camp arrangement is a tussle of wills.

EXHAUSTING!!!!!

The really, really depressing thing is that someone has put this person in charge of children! And everyone here, EVERYONE, every other teacher — even Ian who knows better — just backs away! What if something serious happened? What if she wanted to do something really loony?

Beginning to see how SERIOUSLY ill-prepared this all is. Like those disastrous school trips where people get lost in the snow and aren't even dressed for a rainy day.

Murothi dropped the notebook on the table. He unzipped the tent and stepped outside, drawing a deep breath of the clear night air. A path of moonlight shafted between the trees, and Mungai crossed it, acknowledged him with a brief lift of his stick, merged back into the dark.

Murothi went back in, and took up Anna's drawings. He had already studied the undisguised fury of the girl's cartoons, particularly one of Miss Strutton behind a table spread with little boxes. Each box was labelled: Clever, Stupid, Winners, Losers. Tiny figures peered out of some. He recognised a smug Candy, a supercilious Sean. And it took little effort to detect Anna, Matt, Silowa, Joe, fighting their way out of a 'Losers' box while a giant, snarling Miss Strutton tried to push the lid down on them.

He sat down on the bed, leafing to and fro through the pages. He let his mind wander loosely. Since the events a few hours ago with Sean, he'd seen these drawings in a different kind of light – recognised the particular savagery of Anna's depiction of Sean.

It told Murothi a hidden story – that Anna was the victim of some sort of very personal encounter with this boy, and it had rooted a deep, instinctive fear in her. And anger. The others did not know about it, not even Joe. This, Murothi was also certain about. Even in the strangled mood of this camp someone would have told the police about it, if they'd known. Anna had kept it to herself. He was getting a strong impression of this girl: not one to drag others into her battles, yet, from what Ian Boyd and the students said, not slow to take on the battles of others.

He focused his mind on her sketchbook again. On the last page there was a drawing of a skull. No cartoon, this – detailed, and careful. Not a modern skull, he could tell now that Otaka had explained to him, and anyway, Anna had labelled it: 'Burukanda boy – 1.5 million years old'.

Not bad, is it? Véronique had said when he showed her Anna's drawing, sitting by the fire earlier. *This girl has a talent, certainly. We have a plaster cast of this skull at Burukanda, Murothi. The original is in the museum back in Ulima. It was the first very significant fossil find in this region, twenty years ago. You see here the famous discoverer!* and she'd put a hand on Otaka's shoulder.

Ah, in my energetic youth, Otaka had smiled, with a lift of the eyebrow. *Silowa is very proud of me. He tells everyone!*

Below the drawing, in the peculiar writing that looked like bubbles, was printed the number 1,000. It was Véronique who had guessed its meaning suddenly: *You know what I think that is, Murothi? The prize for the Burukanda competition! It is worth that in English money.*

Eee-ee! A very large pot! Murothi had retorted. *For a children's competition?*

Ah, no. I have not explained properly. The competition is a big, national one: the Burukanda Award, for undergraduate and graduate archaeology students. Winners can use it to help pay for their studies. Here, it pays for two years. The students at Chomlaya camp are being given the chance to enter the competition too, to help give their visit a focus, you see. But of course they will not win this main money prize. It would not be appropriate for them to get such money – it is for students in this country. There will be other rewards for their effort, to encourage them.

But, thought Murothi now, looking at it again, Anna has written it down. If that is what the figures mean –

A conversation with Ella flashed into mind, prompting him to turn to the journalist's notebook. Finding what he sought, he contemplated it for perhaps the twentieth time. At the top of a page, Charly had scrawled: *FOOTPRINTS*. Underneath, in fat quotation marks, *'In the history of the world, the history of the human race is no more than the blink of an eye.'* Beside it was something Ella called a 'doodle'. The notebook was full of these, tucked here and there in the margins: little patterns, stick figures, words decorated with curls. Charly, Ella said, always did these when she was thinking or listening hard.

This one looked to Murothi like stick people having a stick fight. But Ella had seen the figures were holding long bones with nobbles at each end, and managed to read the scribble up the side: THE BATTLE OF THE BONES.

Oh, Véronique had exclaimed, when he showed her, *I remember Charly doing that. Look, Otaka! It was while she was asking about the entry rules for the Burukanda Award, yes?* and Otaka had agreed.

Something here I should be seeing. Every time he looked at it again during this night, this thought niggled at Murothi. But he could not translate the feeling into fact, nothing he could *grasp*, or *do* something with.

Frustrated, he went outside again. Dim lamps marked the perimeter of the camp, and the embers of the dying campfire glowed at its heart. Further out, by the police tents, a single light fell on someone leaning against a vehicle, and inside the tent occupied by Ian Boyd a lamp silhouetted the shape of someone sitting against the canvas. Otherwise, there was no movement, and for a moment Murothi could not detect the helicopter engines either. Then he concentrated his hearing and found the distant hum amidst the light wind sighing through the web of trees.

Does the argumentative Miss Strutton manage to sleep tonight? Earlier, after the incident in Ella's tent, she had looked like a balloon, pricked and collapsed, staring at Sean. Not a single word of protest as Ian Boyd took control. But Murothi had no illusions – she would bounce back into shape by the morning. A flare of vengeful anger had him wishing again that he had grounds to arrest the woman now – just to wipe away the self-satisfied, *dangerous* confidence in her own rightness.

A different thought slipped sideways into his head. Charly made this doodle, this 'Battle of the Bones' scribble, at Burukanda, talking to Véronique and Otaka and showing them Anna's sketchbook. That meant she had the notebook with her *the night before the disappearances*. The missing students were undoubtedly in the camp at that time, at supper with others.

So, he thought, Charly returns to the camp the following morning, and finds the students gone. *Then* she puts the books below the rock, where Joe and Ella and Samuel find them.

Then she goes away herself. And disappears.

Concentrate, Murothi. *Think, think* ... It says something about this woman's frame of mind. She is not panicking. *She does not fear the students are lost.* She is not afraid for them.

She *does* know where they are ...

Frustration flared again. If the intrusive Miss Strutton had not taken Joe's camera, there might be photographs to help the boy's memory. As it was, there was only one picture, taken by Zak, and that had prompted nothing new for Joe when he was shown it.

Quickly Murothi went back into the tent, sifted through everything till he found the photo, scrutinised it under the lamplight. Ella had insisted it was important, from the beginning she'd said so. And of course she was right: Silowa and Anna, on the grass, Charly *appearing* to walk past, but now it was clear she was joining them: talking about what Silowa held on the palm of his hand, that small object that seemed to seal the English girl and the African boy in a shared absorption. A fossil. Possibly even that fragment that Otaka had shown him ...

Wearily he passed a hand across his eyes. They stung with the strain of reading in poor light. More and more his head ached. Fatigue dulled his brain. He craved sleep.

He fought his thoughts into focus again: the fossil, the Burukanda Award; Charly checks the entry rules, Anna writes down the prize. Can this all be only about some plan to enter the competition?

'No!' Ella had said. 'Charly didn't like all that! She says it here, and here and here. Look, she says *It makes me furious to see students actually beginning to bicker about who should be allowed to even enter the competition!*'

Ella was right again: yes, Charly's writings resonated with her dislike of the rivalries brought by Miss Strutton into the world of the camp. Véronique had said to him, 'Charly sees us all dig, dig below the skin of Africa, uncovering the origins of us all, our common ancestors! The students see it. The teachers see it. She says to me that it speaks loudly of the sameness of us all. We have the same roots! Everyone begins here: the cradle of mankind! Instead there was this Miss Strutton who finds every way she can to make all these little ranks: me big, you little; me clever, you stupid; me special, you ordinary. And there is no one who stops her!'

Murothi drank more water. He walked up and down the

tent. He lay down. He let his mind drift. *Find the road you have not walked before, Murothi.*

Charly leaves the camp without telling anyone. *Ella* says this is strange: if Charly was going away, she would say so. *Ella* says her sister has a strong sense of safety. She does not take stupid risks. Murothi, listen to Ella *hard*. She knows her sister. There has been *wisdom* in everything she says . . .

So, Charly goes away without telling anyone.

It means . . . what?

That she is not *going away*. She is not moving *far*. She is staying *within the usual limits of movement round the camp.*

He sat up. Be careful, Murothi: there is no proof she went to the students, that she is with them now. *Joe* does not remember her with them.

But there is a bond between this woman and these children. Everything points to this.

All day, your thoughts have been on the young ones, Murothi. On Joe, Silowa, Anna, Matt.

Think again, Murothi. Think only of the journalist.

Think of Charly. Think of Ella's knowledge of Charly. *Follow them.*

He left the bed quickly, and turned up the light. He sat down, and, again, began rereading.

*

Joe started awake, gasping. His breathing was huge. A roaring filled his ears, like the thunder of a waterfall, his heart drummed, the pounding so loud that the darkness boomed, swelled, gigantic, like the pulse of the earth, like his chest would burst . . .

He sucked in air, jerked upright.

Ella stirred and mumbled, but didn't wake. He sat beside her, chest heaving, till the pounding eased and only her soft breathing filled the dark.

After a minute he stretched against her warmth, letting drowsiness numb him again.

He began to dream.

In the dream he is outside. Light just touches the world, coaxing pinks and browns and greens from the grey.

Around flows a sea of movement. Animals throng to the drum of hooves and the beat of wings. Animals and birds fill the plain and the sky in a limitless moving tide.

Mud oozes between his toes. The tracks of Silowa and Anna and Matt stretch away, cross, separate, loop together. The footprints of a thousand animals pace beside.

The lion treads with him. Heavy maned head swings with the sway of huge shoulders. The leopard pads behind. The eagle soars, the snake lifts and coils, and a thousand birds spiral away . . .

The land is dry. Stones prick his feet. The footprints of Anna and Matt and Silowa curl on through the dust . . .

Then Joe was awake and outside, and didn't know how he had got there. It was still night; a pale silvering wrapped tents and trees and the spaces in between, and a stillness without breath of wind or faintest animal scuffle.

Ella, pushing out of the tent, came beside him, anxious.

'I think it was a dream,' he said. 'Just . . . don't know –'

'The same dream? Like before?'

'It's light . . .' It seeped over him as he stood there. But it was beyond him to put words to the weave of sound and touch and smell. It was like a texture in the air, and the other dream, the darkness fired with colour, galloping, flying, writhing, as if the animals of the day leapt through the night with him too.

He shuddered, and Ella ventured, 'What if you're remembering, Joe? What if it's not *dreaming?*'

He stared at her, white-faced, stricken. 'I haven't been anywhere like the places I'm seeing!'

'But you don't know, do you? You don't remember.'

He looked away, and at the edge of vision something else moved, brought a twist of vicious shock.

She saw him flinch.

He said quickly, to ward it off, 'Also, it's like I keep getting this . . . picture . . . feeling . . . It's in your sister's tent, and I don't know why, because she wasn't there, she went to Burukanda, so why would we go to *her* tent?'

'You told the inspector?'

'Yeah, and we looked, but it's not much good if I don't know why, or if it's true, or what we did after.' He said it angrily, but he was not angry with her, and she did not respond.

Then it hit him: Matt, doubled-up, *retching*, Anna running . . .

He said quickly, not to lose it, 'Matt was being sick, Anna was holding him!' Nausea rose in his own stomach: nausea and a blind fury, and he saw clearly – that this picture was not in Charly's tent after all, but his own, the one he shared with Matt.

'Wait, wait . . . we *left* our tent, went to Charly's to get away from something . . . But there's nothing in ours, *nothing* . . .'

'Let's go and look again,' she pleaded. 'And in Charly's. We can't just leave this, when you've remembered a bit of something. *Joe?*'

'Yeah,' he said. 'Yeah – now!'

*

He swung his torch across the empty beds, Matt's pack, the floor, the canvas walls.

'Work it through,' Ella urged. 'You ate supper. You left the canteen. You came back here?'

He said, carefully, 'Anna went to her tent. I remember that. She wanted to be in before Candy and Janice, because they were doing this stupid thing, holding it closed from inside so she couldn't get in, putting a dead baboon spider –'

The memory hit him: Matt, pushing into their own tent. Matt backing out. His face covered in something – dark, it gleamed wetly in the torchlight, and Matt was stumbling away, vomiting, and Joe's own torch was swinging up, catching the swaying net, the dripping chopped-up mass, the slit, spewing entrails, glistening.

He sat down with a thump.

'What?' she said. 'What, what?'

'They killed the snakes. They chopped them up. They saw us looking at them up in the ravine and they thought it'd be fun to kill the snakes and put them in a net and hang them in the tent for us to walk into. Matt did that, he walked right in, all over his face. There were these buzzing flies on the stickiness, and it was just a little family of snakes –'

Ella could think of nothing to say. She looked up at the ridge pole of the tent. She shone her torch down, at the groundsheet. Nothing. All scrubbed away, clean, innocent.

'And Charly was at Burukanda and Sir was in Lengoi and there was only Strutton here, and those other two: Hopper and Sharp, who never do anything –'

'So – what?' Ella put in, trying to think straight, to help. 'You left and went to Charly's tent? You thought they wouldn't look for you there?'

Morning, light coming – he saw it clearly suddenly –

'Silowa picked up the bag.'

'What bag?'

'Tools.'

'What for?'

'Digging. We were going to dig –'

'Here's the deal,' Anna'd said. 'It's a team thing, right? We're going to enter that Award even though Miss says we can't because we're Silowa's team, and he's going to win and we're going to help him and he's going to do something perfect with the prize. Look, I could do this on my own, but we could all do it. And we get Charly too, so she can be the proof it was him and us and she can tell them it's true.'

'What you on about, what's "it"? What's true?' Joe'd demanded, confused.

'Look, Silowa's found it, and he says he knows there's more, lots and lots. So we'll help him get it, and then Charly can take it to Burukanda and get them to look at it. We won't let anyone else know, so they can't spoil it, or steal it, or break it, or say we didn't do it. And Silowa will win and then – see – Silowa wins the thousand pounds, right? Then he and Ndigi can go back to school and do three more years and get their exams, and after –'

'Ella,' Joe breathed, very slowly, very carefully, in case he lost it again, 'I remember where we went.'

Murothi read and slept and woke and slept again, and when he woke finally, all the mountains of words and thoughts and questions had fallen away and he knew what he was looking for. Not *why* or *when*, but *where*. Not where they were now, but where they had *begun*, and he got up quickly, and one by one searched the sketchmaps, the doodles, the labels.

And there, on the sketchiest map of all – no more than a few squiggles in a page of writing – he found it. It was a small mark: the kind Charly used to indicate places where she'd taken photos or made sketches, or just sat and looked. This particular mark had appeared to Murothi to be a small square with a cross inside it.

Now, imagining Ella's eyes reading it, he saw it for what it was: two tiny stick figures holding bones. A replica of the Battle of the Bones drawing. And it was placed beyond the ravine, beyond Charly's place where the notebooks had been found. On this side of the ridge, below the rocks, along the stream, some way to the east of the camp.

third day: footprints

new dawn

Sunrise of the third day: the first rays fired the horizon and streaked across the land, striking the south-eastern face of Chomlaya. In the warming light, the colossal slabs seemed to stretch, as if they woke and drew breath. An advance guard of baboons foraging beyond their territory bounded along ledges and gullies and froze at the sight of tents below. Then they plunged down into the trees, provoking screeching displeasure among resident birds and monkeys.

In the human camp across the stream a bustle of sudden movement echoed them.

Murothi, Charly's notebook in one hand and a map in the other, was walking out to open plain. Every ten paces or so he looked back. He was trying to get the angle right, to see past the bulging tilt of the cliff to the east of the camp. He wanted sight of the rocks beyond, where they folded back on themselves in the stretch where, on her sketchmaps, Charly had placed her Battle of the Bones mark. All of this was out of sight to him from closer in, near the tents.

The air was dewy and warm. Drifts of mist stroked the

ground, and on the high precipices it wisped and curled, veiling corners and angles. Yet, as he reached the right vantage point some distance out, the rising sun seemed to part the steamy vapour, like a hand drawing a curtain aside. He was gripped by a sense of portent, of imminent events, so violent that his heart pounded, and a fire of energy shot through him. He broke into a run back towards the camp, to call the sergeant, constables, rangers, Joe, Ella – to *get started*. Ten minutes had passed since the sun had tipped the horizon.

But already Sergeant Kaonga was rushing from the police tents; Joe and Ella were calling; even Véronique and Otaka's Land Rover bumped its way from the night's resting place. As he neared, he could hear Joe, *I remember, I remember, we went there, over there, I remember, I remember!* and saw him point in exactly the direction of the place marked by Charly.

It was a scene replayed endlessly in Joe's head. Always it reached the same point and jammed, and started again. *Silowa lifting something from the ground; the stab of a cry, like a piercing note from Matt's pipe, but it wasn't, because Matt was with him . . .* The picture splintered, started afresh: *Silowa kneels, raises it from the burning soil, above, the ear-splitting raucous call . . .*

In the luminous dawn air the scream came again. Ella jerked her head up, looking, and then Joe knew it wasn't memory, but real, its echo reverberating from the pinnacles of the upper rock.

'Where is it?' he demanded, searching the sky.

'There,' she told him, pointing. Spread wings floated dark towards the sunlit crest.

'That is the eagle,' said Véronique, jumping from the vehicle as it rolled to a stop. 'And there is the partner.' She shaded her eyes, following a speck disappearing and reappearing against darker and paler bands of rock. 'There is a pair living here . . .'

Urgently Joe insisted, 'It's what I keep hearing, and just before, Silowa – I don't know, somewhere there –' the story spilled from him fast, incoherent.

Ella, who had managed to grasp most of it, translated, 'See, they went to Charly's tent to get away from the snakes, and they were going to win the competition so Silowa could go back to school, and they went secretly because they didn't want anyone to spoil it or do more horrible things like killing the snakes.'

'Joe, Ella, this is very good, very good,' said Murothi, his mind working overtime to unpick the tale from the incomprehensible torrent and his chest heaving from the run back to camp. 'Joe, show me, this is where you were going?' He had taken the boy's arm and steered him firmly towards the

Land Rover. He spread the notebook and map on the bonnet. Swiftly he explained to them both: Charly's map, the Battle of the Bones sketch.

Joe looked at it all, silently. And then suddenly he looked up at Murothi with such delight in his face that Murothi's heart lifted with a flip of real hope.

The sergeant arrived among them. 'Sir, it is DC Meshami calling! Hoi, he has discovered something! The thing in Matt's hand when they lift the boy from the rock, this thing the climbers tell us about last night? It is not his music pipe! It is old, old! A flute – bone – *old bone*. The DC has flown it to Burukanda, and Mr Peter there says it is from the leg of the eagle! He has seen one like this in France, from the bones of vultures. More than 30,000 years old! And Sir, Sir,' the policeman surged on, 'we hear the report now – strange, strange things!' He shook his head, sucked in breath, 'This is the way it is: the climbers cross over the place where Matt was found, and he is not there, then in just a second, no more, just one second, the helicopter sees him. The climbers are still only fifty metres away! So he has come, *Phut*, out of the ground! This is the only answer! So in the night they have put more people down on the top and they search everything. They find holes, small, filled with bushes. They do not see them from the air. But still there is nowhere for Matt to hide away. A big mystery! Yet they will go on, on, on!' He finished, and grinned triumphantly at Murothi.

They digested this, and Véronique said, 'Peter knows his stuff, Murothi. He is one of the foremost experts in prehistoric artefacts. If he says it is a flute made from fossilised bone of an eagle, then that is what it is. We definitely conclude these children have found something . . .'

'We did, we did,' said Joe, '*Silowa* found it and we went to help him dig it out, but it wasn't a pipe!'

A calming hand on Joe's shoulder, Murothi surveyed the visible sweep of the rock. He indicated the map. 'Sergeant Kaonga, the two boys were discovered *here* and *here* – I have got the positions right?'

They all gathered closer, studying the two crosses Murothi had marked. The sergeant murmured his assent. Musing, Murothi traced the way with one finger: in order, moving eastwards from the tents, you came round the encircling curve of the cliffs, encountering the big ravine, and crossing it. Then on round, to where the overhanging crags ended in a promontory formed from tumbled boulders. This was the point where the ridge turned away from the camp, folding back in a north-easterly direction for a mile or two. Moving along it, you came to the place where Joe had appeared, but in a gully half-way down and on the far side of the ridge. And then even further to where yesterday afternoon Matt had been spotted high on the summit.

Beyond all of this, Chomlaya continued in a series of snaking curves for another five miles.

They followed Murothi's moving finger.

'Look!' Ella had been looking at Charly's map again. 'See! Joe was found there, and Charly's put that Battle of the Bones mark here!' The two positions were roughly in the same region.

But on opposite sides of the rock.

'It seems to me,' said Otaka slowly, 'there is a hidden route up from here to the top and across to the other side. We should look for a place where these children can climb . . .'

'Yes, and they could have got to the top and unhappily fallen into one of these invisible holes we have just heard about!' Véronique shaded her eyes to look at Chomlaya, as if scrutiny alone would reveal all.

'These places have been searched!' the sergeant exclaimed, frustration sharpening his voice. 'When Joe was rescued over there, they looked that side, and then they looked this side! But it is impossible. Steep! Like it is cut with a knife! Chop, chop! A *sharp* knife!'

'Sir, Sir, Mr Boyd, what can we do?' clamouring voices sounded, and Ian Boyd was heading towards them, flanked by a crush of students. 'We got to do something, Sir, we got to help. You said there'd be stuff to do now.' This was Zak speaking. Everywhere was abuzz with activity: Samuel dishing out breakfast of tea, hard-boiled eggs and bread, which they were eating as they assembled, expectant, as if responding to some inaudible call to action.

'What's best, Inspector? Sergeant? Give us your orders,' Ian Boyd asked.

'I will explain the situation for you, Murothi,' Véronique jumped in quickly, seizing the notebook and map. 'And you can rely on Otaka and me to accompany you to this place. You will need trained eyes to help, if these children were searching for fossils, and found something.' To the teacher and the students, she began, 'We do not know exactly what it means yet, but this is what Joe is now recalling . . .'

'We all,' Murothi announced to Joe and Ella, 'together, will go to investigate this place you remember.'

Sergeant Kaonga unclipped the radio from his belt. 'I will tell the helicopters. They will bring climbers to help us,' he announced. 'And I will ask the helicopters to point from the sky to where Joe and Matt were found. So we can mark it from here – I think this is a good idea!'

'Good, yes, good. Where is Mungai?'

'Before light, he goes. He is walking to the north of the rock. He says Silowa will arrive there!'

'Right,' Ian Boyd declared loudly. 'There's a few pairs of binoculars between us. We'll do a detailed scrutiny of the rocks. We can spread right along below. Maybe we can spot the places they could climb. Anything unusual, we'll tell you. OK, everyone. Understood? Four groups. Take a section each.' To the other teachers, also gathering, 'Keith, how about you oversee the first stretch of the ridge? Helen next? Lawrence next, and I'll take the last. Should be able to get reasonable cover over the distance. OK – volunteers to sort out water bottles for all, and don't forget the policemen and the rangers – and Joe and Ella here and Véronique and Otaka. Anyone with binoculars, get them now. Everyone back here in two minutes flat.'

At which point Miss Strutton and Miss Hopper arrived, and were ignored in the enthusiastic rush to get organised.

'Mr Boyd, I want a word,' Miss Strutton called sharply. 'I consider –'

'Time's short, Elisa, we can talk later,' Ian Boyd's voice was brisk, and he was looking beyond her at Sean, who stood apart, watching. The boy's expression was sour.

'Work out where you fit in all this, Sean, and snap into some useful action.' Ian Boyd spoke vigorously. 'Or stay *well* out of it. Lift a finger to get in anyone's way and I'll put you under guard. Make up your mind, eh?'

The boy did not respond. His friends, Carl, Denny, Candy, Janice, heading to join him, looked around with sudden uncertainty.

At Murothi's elbow, Véronique murmured, 'Charly's heart would warm to see this!' She was looking at Miss Strutton and Miss Hopper, and then at all the other teachers busily finalising the binocular teams. 'She said it was like an infection, this hesitancy to argue with this woman or to challenge this horrid boy and his friends. She said there are teachers and children here who know better, who *are* better, but they do nothing! So this little nastiness grows, from silly things to not-so-silly things. But her heart would warm to *this* sight!'

For some minutes, they had followed the base of the ridge. They had passed Charly's place, where she'd hidden the books beneath the boulder. The rough path had petered out, and they were forcing their way through dense, ferny undergrowth bordering the stream. Here the water ran fast down steps of slippery rock, gurgling through narrow channels and splashing into occasional deep, hidden pools.

The boulder-strewn promontory was behind them. They turned along the foot of the rocks running north-east. The force of the sun climbing to their right was fast heating the air to uncomfortable levels.

The expedition had grown. Left in the camp, Constable Lakuya and Likon were manning communications with helicopters and climbers; here on the trek along the rock, Tomis assumed lead of the column while Constable Lesakon, with the radio, brought up the rear. Between the two, Murothi, Joe, Ella, Sergeant Kaonga, Otaka and Véronique pushed along with varying degrees of competency in the steep, treacherous terrain; at every step ledges of rock masked by the ferns threatened to send them sprawling downwards. A little way behind, surprised yelps and nervous laughter came from the binocular teams. There was none of the excited chatter of earlier. The exertion and perils of the route took all of everyone's concentration.

They were equipped, too, with torches and ropes – needed, Tomis and Likon insisted, for looking in dark undergrowth and deep holes.

It was fifteen minutes since they'd left the camp.

The ferny slopes ended, and the stream began to calm through a flat, marshy area of tall grasses and muddy banks. It was easy for Ella to jump to the far side where a stretch of bare earth merged into a slope clothed in low bushes that ran right up to the foot of Chomlaya. For a moment, glimpsing the footprints of Tomis and Murothi ahead of him in the drying mud, a fleeting sense of last night's dream assailed Joe. He felt teeming animal life around him. And something else, intangible and dark and full of sound – and then it was lost again. There was only the red earth and the eight of them walking across it.

On the far bank, the sergeant crouched down and spread the map. Ella knelt down with him, putting Charly's notebook open at the page showing the sketchmaps.

'It's the right place,' she said. 'Look, we're on what Charly's labelled the "orange bank", and there she shows the line of Chomlaya, and that's the reedy edges.' The bank was reddish earth cut through by the course of water running off the rock and joining the stream. A broad, shallow gully had formed; roots of trees and bushes protruded from the sides, denuded of soil. The surface, ridged and cracked, was littered with stones.

'Quite recently formed,' commented Véronique, looking round. 'That last storm washed violently through here. See, it has begun to break the bank away!' She pointed at one edge, split and hanging away, creating a narrow chasm. 'Probably the next storm will wear it smooth. All this will just be sludge washed down and filling up the stream.'

Ella stood up and went over to Joe. He was facing Chomlaya. To their right the helicopter hovered above the point where Matt was found. This information had been communicated moments ago on the radio. They had all looked hard at the shape of the ridge, at where it was in relation to where they stood, committing the place to memory. It was at least a mile further along.

Now the helicopter swung towards them, and stopped again. This time it was above the site of Joe's reappearance on the far side of the rocks; above, too, where they now stood in the gully on this side.

Behind, on the far side of the stream, the binocular teams were spreading along, and Ella could hear the flurry of discussion and instruction floating up in a background babble that merged with the restless grumble of the helicopter.

Joe turned, round and round and round, looking. Ella copied. She tried to follow the direction of his gaze. She felt his tension, like heat off his skin.

Then he stopped suddenly, and went forward. A ragged thorn bush leaned from the gully wall. It was anchored in a protruding ledge of soil, though below had been gouged away by the stormwaters. Roots clawed in the air.

Joe moved to the bush. Ella followed.

Below it was a clutter of stones that, if you did not know, would look natural. But if you looked carefully, you could see they had been moved and placed in a rough half-circle round the roots of the bush.

Otaka had been watching Joe. Now he looked where Joe looked. And with a sharp intake of breath, the man squatted down and beckoned Joe to his knees beside him. He motioned Joe to lift the dangling roots. Gently Otaka brushed at the soil in the side of the bank. Earth fell away easily where it had once been disturbed and returned.

Before their eyes, a smooth, pale dome emerged. Otaka continued stroking the earth, gently, patiently, until the whole side of the skull lay revealed, one eye socket looking impassively out at them.

Simultaneously, several things happened. With a long, yelping cry, the eagle dropped from the rock and swooped low, wingbeats whipping the air. The helicopter roared into sight, blasting a gale along the cliff. Bushes flattened. Dust and leaves gusted upwards. Véronique let out a yell, and yanked creepers away from the carpeting layer on the bank beside the gully. 'The propellers blew it up. Look!' she shrieked through the noise.

Below the foliage was a ledge of rock. She pointed to a wobbly-edged oval in the surface. She lifted more leaves: another shape. With one finger she traced a trail of others to one side, and they all saw them then, outlined by the low-angled rays of the sun.

Blankly, they stared. Then, 'Footprints?' breathed Murothi. 'In the *rock*?' His voice was suddenly loud against the receding throb of the engine.

'*We* saw that,' Joe said urgently. 'Silowa called it footprints of the God.' He was gripping Ella's arm so hard it hurt.

Véronique sat back on her heels. 'Otaka, tell about Laetoli!' He was bending over, scanning the marks with concentration.

'Prehistoric footprints,' he responded, not looking up. His voice, like Véronique's, was tight with excitement. 'Thirty years ago they found them in Tanzania.' He straightened. 'More than *three million years* they lay hidden below soil, the tracks of two adults and a child, trapped in the hardened ash of a volcano. Then the soil is eroded away; there they are again, the tracks released to our eyes!'

'Human-like creatures,' Véronique emphasised. 'Striding

across an ancient landscape! Our *ancestors*! An extraordinary find! The Laetoli prints are flanked by animal tracks fleeing the erupting volcano –'

A volley of shouts from the students exploded across the stream, and a crackle on the radio stung the constable into action, jumping away to listen.

Murothi's eyes swung to the rock. Briefly muted by wispy cloud, the sun broke free, drenching Chomlaya in hard, bright light, crevice and ledge, nobble and crack chiselled in black on the gigantic slabs.

'Sir, you have seen something?' demanded the sergeant.

'Only the change in the angle of light.'

'The marks . . . they're going to the rock, they're walking up . . .' Ella, mesmerised by the footprints, recovered her voice, and Murothi followed her gaze, glanced back at the marks, at the crags, at her, and then squeezed her shoulder in agreement.

'Sir, it is the teacher Mr Boyd,' the constable brandished the radio high. 'A girl has climbed a tree down there. She tells that above, up there . . .' he gestured up the gully, 'is a dark place. She thinks it is a *hole* . . .'

'You could move up that way,' Tomis pointed to chunks of fallen rock providing a possible line of ascent.

Decisively, Véronique pulled the creepers over the

footprints and Otaka moved to cover the skull with soil. He dragged a loose branch on top. 'It has waited millions of years for us to meet it, it will wait longer,' he said. 'It is the living who call –'

'Wait,' Joe said. Ella felt the vibration of his heart against her arm, he was hanging on like it was a lifeline. 'It was – See, the *bird* –' he *remembered* speeding darkness, the cry; it jarred through him again. 'Silowa put earth on the skull like that . . . then he went up –' he was tugging Ella towards the rocks, slithering on the loose sand of the gully where it steepened between boulders, his words lost in a spill of dislodged pebbles.

In a few swift strides, Murothi had caught them and had his hand on Joe's shoulder, as if terrified he would dart out of sight.

It took only moments. The lower boulders offered easy stepping places to the higher. From on top you could see a shelf jutting from the cliff, well out of sight from below, reachable from boulders wedged against it. Scrawny bushes clung here and there, and a short distance to their right, the shelf crumbled away.

The dark place seen by the girl in the tree was close. With the angle of the early sunlight, you could just detect the vertical shadows of its upper end, several metres high. Lower down it was curtained by scraggy branches.

'Inspector . . .' Tomis's voice was cautious, but he did not need to say more: the cleft breathed dank air into their faces, promised depth and distance. Tomis pushed the bushes aside. Behind, it widened enough to take the bulk of a man.

Joe felt as if he watched across a great gap of time, a great gap of space. The fluted pinnacles leaned in, the grooves and ridges of the rock moved. Like a shifting of mood, a sense of music, piercing every nerve of his body. In two dream-haunted nights he had heard it, in chaotic half-memory; yesterday it had called to him that Matt was there, was alive.

It called him now, into the heart of the rock.

He bowed through the crack in the cliff, and disappeared.

'Wait!' Murothi shouted, and leapt after him, the rest of them, stooping and pushing through and finding almost at once that they could stand.

They were in a chimney. The crack in the rock was behind them, masked again by bushes on the outside. Sheer walls on the other sides. Above, a canopy of foliage: columns of green light fell through leaves, flecked with gold, spun with spider webs, rippling on their upturned, startled faces.

Sheer walls – except to their right. Here the rock split again into blackness. Through this, Joe had again disappeared.

'Do not go on!' Murothi struggled through.

'It's OK, I know . . .' Joe's words floated back, and were lost in a tumble of echoes.

'We expect caves, but there are none – I spoke too soon,' Véronique's voice echoed, breathy and loud, and at that moment the sergeant switched on a torch and the beam raked ahead, splashing light on Joe vanishing at the end of a long black hole into nothing.

Ella had surged in with the others, and slid to a halt now, walls scraping her shoulder. She felt the rock pressing in, suffocating. Terror merged with a panic that threatened to cripple all other movement – Charly – *anyone* – in here! Joe *lost* again! Her breathing ricocheted off the tunnel like a wild thing stalking her in the gloom.

Murothi and Tomis and the sergeant had forged ahead, out of sight. She jumped as Véronique touched her shoulder. 'It is all right, Ella,' the woman said, 'just breathe slowly. See, they have switched the torches on, they are all right, just beyond, there. Move to the light. Really, my dear, it is all right, it is *all right.*'

A blush of colour filled the end of the tunnel.

Wordlessly, Ella forced herself to obey. One step, another . . . hanging on to the feel of Véronique and Otaka and

Constable Lesakon anchoring her behind.

There was a rush of cold air. They were stepping out into a wave of sound, and there were Joe and Murothi and Tomis and Sergeant Kaonga. Transfixed, wordless, looking up.

'It wasn't dreaming, Ella,' Joe whispered. 'It was *remembering*, like you said.' Above him, two vast red eland galloped on a rocky overhang. A lion paced the wall, a snake coiled from shadows, and everywhere trickles of sound made a web of sighs, lifting his voice into the darkness.

Véronique moved past him, stretched a hand, palm out, towards the wall. Behind the shadows of her spread fingers Ella saw the matching handprints gleaming white amid red and black dots, arrow-heads, cavalcades of lizards that seemed to slither from cracks in the rock.

She looked up. A cat-like yellow figure stretched on the ceiling. It turned its strange, horned head to look down at her.

Recovering himself from awestruck silence, Murothi ventured, 'These paintings are old?'

'Murothi, these are *prehistoric*,' Otaka answered. 'I am not an expert, but I make a guess, more than 20,000 years. No – I will be bold – older! Yes, older, older!' Visible excitement was already supplanting his own hushed astonishment. 'Murothi, my friend, the bone flute comes from these caves – I mean the one Matt was holding when they rescued him yesterday. We must acknowledge now, these children have not climbed *over* the rock; they have passed through its heart!'

Murothi swivelled to face Joe. 'You saw all this? You had torches?'

'I saw – but we didn't have torches, didn't know we were coming here . . .'

'Then how could you see?'

'I . . .' Joe stared round, confused, 'I . . . I just could. And there were voices – there –'

'Water,' said Véronique. 'The sound we can hear is water rushing through other parts of the rock. And the echoes from it. And our own voices travelling back to us.' She gestured to horizontal spaces high up, recesses probing deep into walls, corners and clefts exuding icy darkness.

'No –' Unexpectedly, Joe moved towards a wide, low opening to one side. He began to stoop into it. With a start, Tomis held him back and slipped past. 'Careful, careful!' Cautiously the ranger went in first. Joe followed, and one by one the rest of them too. A few paces in, they had to duck under a low lintel of rock.

They stood up into an immense vaulted space. Torchbeams swung up. A rhinoceros trotted across the heights. Blackness fell away below. A rock-bridge stretched ahead.

'Is it safe to go over?' Murothi's voice was huge in the cavernous gloom. He was assessing the bridge.

'It is broad and solid,' Véronique assured him. 'We can safely pass along its centre.'

The sergeant flicked torchlight down to one side. It revealed the deep, narrowing pit and a riot of colour: red and black and yellow, quivering in the passing beam.

Ella absorbed only the slope into blackness, the rumble of distant sound. She had a picture of squirming holes and bottomless falls, and was clammy with dread, with the effort not to reveal her trembling.

Murothi and Joe stepped on to the bridge. Carefully the others went with them. Lightly, Constable Lesakon touched Ella's arm, gesturing her forward. Nerves turned her legs to lead. She felt her way forward clumsily. But she found that the bridge was indeed broad, the drop much further away than she'd thought. She began to quicken her pace to reach the others.

They had come to a halt, though. Beyond the rock-bridge, the far wall was no wall but a bend in the cave. Out of sight, the floor undulated downwards and divided around a pillar of rock. Both routes dropped sharply away, and in the one to the left, some distance down, Tomis's torch revealed patches of deeper gloom hinting at other openings.

He turned to Joe. 'Which way?'

The hunted look came over Joe's face, and Ella went cold, cold beyond the cold of the caves.

'Joe?' she moved towards him.

Joe glanced at her. Then at the two possible directions. He remembered sound, like a thousand voices in the hollows. He remembered following the sound. He remembered turning and they were no longer there, there was only him, and the dark air threaded with muttering, and nothing else.

Mute, he shook his head. He looked into her face, helplessly.

Murothi shone the torch on his watch. Ten minutes since they'd entered the caves. An hour, now, since dawn.

'Sergeant, Constable, we cannot go further without reporting to the outside. We will have search parties looking for us! If you please, go out now, radio these developments to Likon and Constable Lakuya. Get them to report everything to the helicopters and direct their search immediately above us. And we must have expert help in here. How long till the climbers arrive? Then come back quickly. We must go on, but we set up a clear route for return. We do not get ourselves lost!'

'Yes, Sir, we can use the ropes,' agreed Tomis. 'To mark the route . . . we have six ropes here, we can get more . . .'

'I have explored caves many times, Murothi,' Véronique put in. 'We will lead, Tomis and I, yes? Sergeant Kaonga, I suggest you get the teacher Lawrence Sharp too – he has caving experience.'

Sergeant and constable were already going back across the bridge, the thud of their footsteps resounding across the space.

'Murothi, this is what I think,' Véronique announced. 'Holes on the summit of Chomlaya have eroded into these caves. Rainwater percolates down, you see. In the end the surface collapses. You understand? *This* is how Joe and Matt have climbed out in these far-off places –'

Joe had crouched down, elbows on knees, chin on clenched fists, facing the tunnels burrowing into rock.

Ella squatted beside him. He looked briefly at her again, unsmiling, and away. There was a faint glisten on his cheeks. She felt him lean towards her, warmth from his arm transmitting across the chill cave air.

'Sorry,' he whispered. 'Don't remember. All mixed up. Sorry . . .'

Murothi declared, 'Joe, you have brought us here! That is good! Now we know you came to this place. We know where you and Matt came out. You have told us all this! We will find your friends. It is not your burden. It is not your *fault*.'

Joe nodded. He did not look at the policeman. He wiped the back of his hand across his eyes.

Decisively, Otaka called to Véronique and they began examining the extremities of the cavern: bulges, crevices, platforms of rock, passing to and fro, their voices filling the space with murmuring. It merged with the fall of water, and it seemed to Ella suddenly as if chanting and singing impregnated the rock, as if the dark thronged with life, as if the torchlight flickering across the undulations of the floor was the flame of a kindling fire.

But she was shivering, stiff with cold. 'Let's move, Joe. Let's look too.' She stood, and saw, etched by the shimmer of moving light, trails of marks, long, oval marks, treading into the obscurity in front of her.

She gripped Joe's arm. 'What's that?'

Otaka, passing close by, shone his torch down, and along. He let out a sudden exclamation, knelt. He looked up at Ella. 'Footprints, in dust. They are new! Inspector Murothi!' He moved along, swore under his breath, knelt again, blew gently across a line of marks further away. 'But these are not new. These are hard in the rock.' He stabbed the torch around, 'Different marks, different sizes – four, no five. Véronique, you must see this! The new marks overlay the old! It is a matter of great wonder!'

Murothi came and looked, but he could not take it in. He could think of nothing but five days trapped in this labyrinth. He was eyeing the animals that seemed to leap live from the veins of the rock, as if they flowed from its spirit. He could almost hear the hoofbeats of the eland, the snarl of the leopard.

These children – *lost*, without light, without food, without water, down here?

He tried to still a sudden, rising panic, to organise the facts in his head: *Silowa, Anna, Joe and Matt come to this place at dawn. Together. Possibly Charly follows them in. Thirty-six hours pass, and Joe emerges, just on the other side of the rock. Alone. Another three days pass and Matt is found. In a different place – some way to the east. Now, sixteen more hours had passed . . .*

The children came in together; how did they lose each other? Why? Where, where to look now? Were they all scattered, maybe even deep below in one of these terrible plunging holes?

This endless wait for the sergeant! He snapped his torchbeam on to his watch again. Five minutes since the sergeant and Constable Lesakon left –

Suddenly, loudly, Joe said, 'I don't remember Charly here. I don't. She *wasn't* here.'

'Yes!' cried Tomis from the left-hand tunnel. 'No! I mean, she *was*! See!' He scooped something from the ground and held it up: a leather lace threaded with beads. 'A child gave *this* to her just last week!'

'It *is* hers. She wore it round her neck.' Véronique ran forward to take it. 'I have seen it!'

For Ella everything fused into the mountain of rock pressing down. Like a tomb. She could think of nothing else: Charly, Anna, Silowa, in a tomb. She began to shake, unable to stop.

Beyond the rock-bridge, there was a drumming of footsteps.

Murothi turned to greet the flare of their torches, like a blast of warmth from the sunlit outer-world.

Sergeant and constable burst in, slid to a halt, gasped for breath.

'They are there!' the sergeant yelled.

'Between the helicopter this way and this way!' bawled the constable.

'What are you saying, man?' Murothi roared, knowing, yet not daring to believe.

'Hoi, Sir,' shrieked the sergeant. 'We send the helicopters down. Suddenly they are there!'

'*Anna and Silowa?*'

'And Charly! Anna, Silowa, Charly. *All!*'

'Poof!' a triumphant constable flung his arms up high. 'They have risen from the stomach of earth! Alive!'

Joe and Ella and Murothi emerged from the rift in the cliff, and paused on the ledge. The sun bore down directly, and Ella was assailed by the scorch of the rock at her back, the peppery brush of leaves against her legs, the lichen patterns below her hand as she braced herself. As if warmth and light and life fought to erase for all time the cold terror of the caves.

Across the stream below them, a heady victory chant began, a mad pounding about, slapping hands: *alive, alive, alive, alive*. Birds fled the trees in disgust. Joe stepped from the ledge on to the broad, flat top of the boulders. And then, as if triggered from his state of shock by the tumult, he suddenly whooped and whirled Ella round, and she clung to him, yelling, and Murothi found himself with his arms round both of them, feeling for all the world like a proud father.

Likon and Constable Lakuya, climbing up, met Véronique and Sergeant Kaonga and Tomis and Constable Lesakon scrambling down the gully, and there was a great deal more shoulder-clapping and hand-shaking and guffaws of laughter.

'Out of the gully!' ordered Otaka sternly. 'With your great

fat boots you will destroy the treasure of millions of years!' But he sat high on the boulders, smiling down on them like a benign spirit of the rock. 'Truly,' he remarked to no one in particular, 'this is the place of life.'

'The nurse said that! Pirian,' Ella shrieked. 'In the hospital –'

'Well, your Pirian knows Chomlaya,' returned Otaka. 'The place of birth, the place of life; the place of death and life,' he went on, enjoying himself. 'This is what Chomlaya tells us, eh? We are given the young ones back. *Their* time has not yet come.'

As if in confirmation, the helicopter shot upwards from the summit of the rocks, swung in a wide circle, and flew away towards Nanzakoto and the hospital.

'We will go now to Nanzakoto!' declared Murothi. 'To meet your sister. And Silowa, Anna, Matt. In Nanzakoto,' he said again. 'I will meet them all! Every one!'

Had he ever had such a feeling of contentment in all his life?

Ella and Joe scrambled down into the ferment of excitement, buffeted by the storm of explanation from the students.

'Janey saw the cave! She climbed the tree!' shouted

Tamara, dragging Ella to admire the smooth, unclimbable trunk of the baobab. The first branches spread high, out of reach except to a giant. 'Ant and Zak lifted her up on their shoulders!'

'The tree of Africa,' announced Ian Boyd. 'Probably the oldest living thing in the world. Maybe 25,000 years old. Maybe it was here when those paintings were done! Maybe the artists walked right under this tree.' No one was listening.

'You see, Janey was *meant* to see the caves!' declared Hilary. 'It was *destiny*.' Hilary was into fate and star signs. Janey rolled her eyes in mock despair.

To Ella it didn't sound so mad an idea, now.

'Well, *Inspector* Murothi, success!' Véronique called. Gingerly, he was making his way across the gritty sands of the gully. He had a picture of walking on uncountable treasures underfoot.

He grinned at Véronique. He felt light – light and joyful, and ridiculously carefree. 'A team effort!' he called back. 'Even the disapproving Miss Strutton could be proud of us!'

The air was free of the incessant mutter of engines. Moments ago, this had dawned on him. The rock basked in the returning hum of insects. White clouds of butterflies rose from the reeds, and even wading birds had ventured out on to the mud by the stream.

Murothi stood with Véronique, watching Otaka. The man worked carefully with delicate strokes of a small brush, clearing the soil round the skull. He'd already spotted other fossils embedded in the bank nearby, and marked these with small sticks pushed into the soil.

With her head on one side, Véronique regarded Murothi.

'You see! He will be oblivious to all, Murothi. He will bring Silowa back here. For months these two will dig, dig, dig in this place, to discover its secrets. There is happy work here for years!' She took Murothi's arm. 'But you are a digger too! To find these little marks on these little maps and to know what they told us . . .' she flapped her hand, signifying something beyond her. 'In another life, Murothi, you would be digging the sands of time, like us, I think?'

Murothi was wondering about the creeper-covered bank and its cargo of footprints, still hidden. Who had walked there? When? What had brought them here? And the skull – was it man or woman? Was this the person who had walked on the volcanic ash that hardened to rock – or were the prints from others still sleeping below the land here? And who had left the ancient footprints Ella spied inside the caves?

Such *detective* work – to see their stories in the marks and layers and language of the land!

'It would be a good life,' he said.

'What's happening?' Tamara wanted to know. Everyone was gathering expectantly on the rim of the camp.

'We're going to Nanzakoto – Inspector Murothi and Joe and me,' Ella told her gleefully. 'Any minute the helicopter's coming for us.'

'Matt's conscious,' added Joe. 'Just when Anna and Silowa and Charly got to the hospital, he woke up!'

'Tell them hi from us,' Janey said.

'Yeah, and –' Zak didn't finish, shrugged, charged off on another tack. 'So, you remember, Joe? Why you went off, all secret?'

'Hey, don't!' Janey's elbow dug Zak in the ribs, and she frowned meaningfully.

Joe laughed. 'It's OK,' he said. 'Yeah, it's OK.' He did remember it. But he couldn't put anything in words. After the snakes, in Charly's tent: Matt sick with stumbling into the sad shreds of them, with being afraid to go out and rinse off the bloody bits. *They'll just find us here, you know they will, Anna. Joe, won't they just do something else? We've got to tell –* And Anna, vehement, *Who? Tell who, Matt? Charly's the only one who listens, and she's not here. No, we'll show them. Joe? Silowa's going to win that competition, right? Silowa? We'll go and dig out*

that skull you've seen, and we'll stay out there till Charly gets back,

and we'll tell no one, not one single person except Charly –

'You coming back, Ella?' Tamara was asking. 'With Charly?'

Ella looked round at the rock, the tents, the arid, yellowing plain stretching away. How strange, the speed of everything! Nothing coloured by terror any more. Even Sean's violence was a distant memory. His friends seemed caught up in the elation along with everyone else, though Sean was nowhere to be seen. As if he had no place.

'Yes,' she said. 'When Charly's OK, we'll come back –'

'And this I told you!' Samuel's voice boomed happily in her ear. 'Your sister will return to ask more questions. Have I not said this? And was I not right?'

'The walls of the house do not tell what is going on inside,' Samuel said dourly to Murothi. He was looking at Miss Strutton. 'When the newspapers come, she will be in charge! So that when people ask who has done this rescue, she can scoop from the pot!'

'Who cares!' Ian Boyd retorted lightly. 'May she enjoy her own little competition without us. The rest of us will go to Kasinga tomorrow to help build that schoolroom – get on with something *useful*.'

'Murothi, we expect to see you back,' shouted Véronique, arm in arm with Otaka.

In response, Murothi raised a hand, and to Likon and Tomis, standing with them.

Constable Lesakon and Constable Lakuya had pushed their caps back to a daring angle. The sergeant walked with a spring in his step.

'DC Meshami will meet you, Sir,' he declared. 'He is very happy. Mungai is very happy too. I have given orders to take him to Nanzakoto hospital straightaway to see his cousin. You will see him there. And I am to tell you that the families from England will reach Nanzakoto tonight. A good job, Sir! The *Minister* will be very pleased.' He put his sunglasses on; they flashed merrily.

'A very good job, Sergeant Kaonga. We make a good team, all, eh?' Murothi shook the sergeant's hand energetically, then the constables'. In mock solemnity, they stood briskly to attention, saluting. Murothi laughed.

The pilot swung the helicopter along the full sinuous length of Chomlaya. Ella had asked if they could, and Murothi wanted to say goodbye. He was thinking about his first sight of the rock, how he'd felt its unchanging watchful presence. How he'd wondered about its stories.

He knew the answer now. He had encountered some of its secrets. But what of others, as unfathomable as the caves and tunnels of the rock themselves? Joe still could not tell him why they'd left the skull and climbed to the caves, could not say how they'd known those caves were there. And for all Murothi's policeman's instinct, it was not a question he wanted to probe too deeply. He'd *felt* it himself – that precision of light, that resonance of sound. Had he not felt his own gaze drawn to the rock moments before the cleft was seen?

But the children, all of them, had been the ones to *see*.

Now the rock slept in the sun. People dwindled; antelope and zebra and giraffe became strokes of shadow, like charcoal on a sweeping yellow canvas.

Joe was thinking that in all the questions he would have to face, there were some things he couldn't ever explain. We didn't *follow* Silowa. We all walked separately into the caves. Separately. And together.

He was not stupid enough to try to say it. But it was true. In the caves he'd heard the murmur of water, bubbling through rock, just as Véronique said. But he'd heard other music too.

No way could he try to *tell* anyone!

Well, maybe Ella. She sat in front beside the pilot. He thought of his first sight of her, propped in the window of the hospital room. Pale and scared. Obstinate. He knew that look on her face now. Obstinacy. No, he wouldn't get away without trying to explain it to Ella.

Resting her forehead against the window, a kaleidoscope of pictures was spinning through Ella's mind. The caves, the camp, returning. *Joe.*

And Pirian. The nurse's kindness. I'll go to the clinic again, and help her, Ella thought. When Charly's resting.

Her notebook lay on her lap like a remnant of another time. *Charly*, she imagined writing, *we're flying to you, as fast, as fast as we can. In an hour I'll be there, where you are. I'll see you, see you, SEE YOU!*

She felt Joe's gaze and looked round. She smiled. He smiled back. And Murothi, seeing the exchange, smiled at both of them, but they were too absorbed to notice.

Now they had reached the eastern end of Chomlaya. The pilot looped the helicopter round and began its return. They reached the camp, swung lower in a final farewell, and turned for Nanzakoto.

Murothi's memory flashed to Likon. *Burukanda people will come to look at the caves*, the ranger had said. *And the newspapers will come. And then the visitors. Chomlaya will get a headache!*

Let me say this, Tomis had answered, *Chomlaya is old and wise enough to give them the headache.*

Murothi could almost hear the groan of the settling rock. In the wake of the helicopter, the eagle soared from the crags and vanished against the white brilliance of the sky.

To Ella and Joe, Murothi said, 'It is told that the souls of men return in the form of birds and snakes. Perhaps we have been led in all things by the soul of Silowa's father.'

He did not really mean it. And yet, at the same time, he did.

postscript

TEENAGERS' ORDEAL REVEALS PREHISTORIC SECRETS

From our science correspondent

Four teenagers have discovered prehistoric paintings estimated to be nearly 30,000 years old in deep caves in Chomlaya Ridge. They have also found ancient hominid fossils taking us millions of years back into our prehistory.

The students and an English journalist have been the subject of an extensive ground and air search since they disappeared without trace from their camp almost a week ago. Two of the youngsters had reappeared, days apart, in different locations. In an extraordinary turn of events, the explanation for the disappearances materialised at the same time as the last two students and the journalist struggled to the surface. It appears they were led out by following the vibration of helicopter engines, which had been directed to the right location by the searchers inside the caves.

Remarkably, everyone is unhurt, except for shock and the ravages of hunger and dehydration.

'This discovery must be laid entirely at the door of these young people,' said palaeontologist, Dr Otaka Ngolik, one of the party who entered the caves in search of the missing students. 'And its rediscovery to their schoolmates who detected the rift in the rock that led us to the caves.'

It is still not known what prompted the students and the journalist into the caves in the first place. The entrance is a climb of some thirty metres from the ground, and completely hidden by rock falls and foliage growth. Nor is it understood how they became separated inside. Memories remain patchy and confused. Doctors are blaming the scale and trauma of their ordeal.

PREHISTORIC TREASURE TROVE

The caves and long decorated galleries pass deep into the rocks. Hominid fossils from widely different periods have been found both inside and on the immediate approach outside.

Archaeologist Véronique Mézard, also one of the first into the caves, told us, 'Preliminary investigation of the rock strata and sediments where fragments of three skulls have been found – as well as rib pieces, teeth, jaw bones, vertebrae and pelvis, which appear to come from six individuals – suggest they are each of widely different prehistoric periods.

One is very similar to a find made in Chad, dating from between six and seven million years ago. And one at least is possibly even older, taking us much closer than we have ever been to our common ancestry with chimpanzees – somewhere between seven and eight million years ago. It will be a long time before we understand the sequence of these finds, let alone how such layering of hominid history has become concentrated in this one place. Analysis of the paintings alone, which are much more recent, will keep everyone busy for many years to come. And who knows what else may be spread through the caves. But all this will undoubtably immeasurably enlarge our conception of the evolution of the human family tree, and this continent as the birthplace of all humankind.'

The caves are already yielding a tantalising horde: stone tools, lamps, hearths, painted pebbles, and much more recent artefacts, including bone flutes and other musical instruments, some in very remote nooks and crannies. Dr Peter Koinege, Director of the National Archaeology Foundation and an expert in prehistoric artefacts, said, 'People walked, ran and danced in these caves. And perhaps they sang. There is an extraordinary resonance inside, as you find in the highly decorated deep-cave systems of Ice Age Europe.'

Dr Otaka Ngolik told us, 'It is like a wonderful gift to us, such knowledge of our universal human heritage. We will speculate for many years as to how single individuals from widely differing times, have left their bones here. Perhaps, as the legends of Chomlaya say, our ancestors truly did come here when the time of their death-call came. Strangest of all, perhaps, is that in the floor of one cave are the footprints of four children, overlaid by those of an adult. They are very old prints, set hard in ancient sediments, but one cannot help but compare the events of these past few days, when four young people and an adult walked right through the heart of Chomlaya to emerge the other side.'

LOCAL STUDENT WINS MAJOR BURSARY

Silowa Asumoa, 14, leader of the group of students who discovered Chomlaya Caves, has been awarded an education bursary by The National Archaeology Foundation. It will cover six years, to allow him to continue his secondary education and subsequent training as a palaeontologist. The foundation has also announced that the other young people involved, Joe Wilson, Anna Benham and Matt Fisher, will be brought out from England later this year to take part in further exploration of the cave system they discovered. The invitation has also been extended to Ella Tanner, the younger sister of the English journalist, for playing such a significant part in the rescue.

The English journalist, Charlotte Tanner, who endured the five-day ordeal lost in the caves with Silowa, said, 'From the beginning Silowa was fascinated by the myths around this rock – particularly the widespread legend of a god's footprints on the rock. He has such a passion to know – he fired up all of us to share his search for answers.'